PUFFIN BOOKS

WORZEL GUMMIDGE AGAIN

Worzel Gummidge, in case you don't know, is the scarecrow of Ten-acre Field at Scatterbrook Farm; a regular, turnip-headed, broomstick-legged, straw-stuffed scarecrow; and, being a scarecrow, what he knows about the earth and the air and the sky, is not at all what you and I or any ordinary human being might expect. What do you suppose struck him as just right for a hair brush? Why, a hedge-hog! And when he kept school, what do you suppose he taught young scarecrows (when there were any)? And what was Gummidge's idea of being a handyman? Read and find out for yourself.

There are not very many funny books written for children, but this is one to call forth chuckles and gurgles at every page. Ages? From about nine upwards – you're never too old to enjoy Gummidge.

Also in Puffins: *Worzel Gummidge*, *Worzel Gummidge and Saucy Nancy*, *The Trials of Worzel Gummidge*, *The Television Adventures of Worzel Gummidge*, *More Television Adventures of Worzel Gummidge* and *Worzel Gummidge at the Fair*.

GW00729122

WORZEL GUMMIDGE
AGAIN

Barbara Euphan Todd

PUFFIN BOOKS

Puffin Books, Penguin Books Ltd, Harmondsworth, Middlesex, England
Penguin Books, 625 Madison Avenue, New York, New York 10022, U.S.A.
Penguin Books Australia Ltd, Ringwood, Victoria, Australia
Penguin Books Canada Ltd, 2801 John Street, Markham, Ontario, Canada L3R 1B4
Penguin Books (N.Z.) Ltd, 182–190 Wairau Road, Auckland 10, New Zealand

—

First published 1937
Published in Puffin Books 1949
Reprinted 1952, 1976, 1977, 1979, 1980 (three times)

—

—

Made and printed in Great Britain
by Richard Clay (The Chaucer Press) Ltd,
Bungay, Suffolk
Set in Monotype Baskerville

Dedicated to
J. G. B.

CONTENTS

—

CHAPTER I

GUMMIDGE'S HAIRBRUSH

—

IT was early September, and John and Susan had come to spend the last fortnight of their summer holiday at their old nurse's home in Scatterbrook. She was married now, but her sister, Mrs Braithewaite, was still at the farm, so was Farmer Braithewaite and so was the tortoiseshell cat. Everything, or nearly everything, looked exactly the same. Everything smelled exactly the same too, and the scent of dough rising in big earthenware crocks before the kitchen fire gave them a hungry feeling. Out-of-doors the smells were different because their last visit had been made in the Spring when moss and bricks were damp, and hens walked in a finicking way through mud and even the hay in the lofts had a faint musty tang about it. Now the lavender was dry on the hedge and the straw smelled hot and summery.

Susan wrinkled up her nose and sniffed as soon as she and John were left alone together.

'I wonder if we shall see Worzel Gummidge,' she said. 'Oh! I do hope he hasn't left Scatterbrook.'

Worzel Gummidge was the scarecrow who used to live in Ten-acre Field and scare away the rooks when he was not doing more important business of his own. John and Susan had made friends with him in the Spring and had met a lot of other queer scarecrows – Upsidaisy who had three legs that had once belonged to a milking-stool, Hannah Harrow (she was always limp and sad because she was stuffed with sawdust and the mice had been at her) and Earthy Mangold who

had married Worzel Gummidge last Spring, just before
John and Susan left Scatterbrook.

'I don't think he'd ever go away for long,' said John.
'I think he'd always come back or something.'

'Yes,' agreed Susan. 'He'd be an awfully bad packer.
Not that he's got many clothes to pack, of course.'

'He's got his bottle-straw boots, and the Squire's
trousers and the Vicar's coat and the string braces,' said
John.

'But only one of each. And if you've only got one of
each there's nothing to pack.'

'Oh! all *right*,' said John.

Just then Mrs Braithewaite called them in to tea –
new scones, clover honey, milk, and dark home-made
cake that was soggy in the middle and tasted of toffee.
Farmer Braithewaite came clumping into the kitchen,
told them how much they had grown, and promised to
show them the new calf. But they didn't want to see the
new calf just then because they were longing to go in
search of Worzel Gummidge, the scarecrow of Scatterbrook.

Mrs Braithewaite was most provokingly slow as she
knelt by the big trunk on the landing, and handed
shirts and shorts and pyjamas for John to take to his
room; and then paused to examine Susan's new cotton
frocks and Sunday coat. The trouble was that she would
not let them go for a walk until she had unpacked their
country shoes and oldest clothes. These, of course, were
at the bottom of the trunk.

'More haste less speed!' warned Mrs Braithewaite
as Susan collided with John and sent hairbrushes and
books tumbling down the stairs.

At last she let them go, but even then she called them
back from the gate to warn them not to be late for
supper, and Farmer Braithewaite told them not to

go through the long meadow because of the bull.

They stopped by Mrs Kibbins' cottage and looked over the wall.

'Do you remember the time Mrs Kibbins bought Gummidge at the jumble sale?' said Susan, 'and used him as a scare-*sparrow?*'

'And do you remember the Fair and that awful Aunt Sally of his?' said John. 'And his braces?'

'Made of tarred string,' interrupted Susan. 'And the robin's nest in his pocket and the way he used Mrs Robin as a handkerchief. I wonder if he's grown at all.'

'Scarecrows don't grow,' said John. 'Scarecrows are much more likely to shorten. People might chop bits off their broomstick legs.'

'Don't be horrid,' said Susan in a very shocked voice. 'Besides all scarecrows don't have broomsticks for legs. Upsidaisy had milking-stool legs. And Earthy Mangold –'

'I wonder,' interrupted John, 'I wonder if Earthy likes being married to Gummidge. She was quite the nicest of all the lady scarecrows we met at the party. I didn't care much for Hannah.'

They might have stood by Mrs Kibbins' wall for a long time, reminding each other of all the queer ways of Worzel Gummidge, and warming their hands on the hot lichen-covered bricks if Mrs Bloomsbury-Barton had not chanced to come along the road.

Now Mrs Bloomsbury-Barton was the only person who did not seem to suit Scatterbrook at all. She wore Londony clothes and feathery hats and high-heeled shoes.

'Why!' exclaimed Mrs Bloomsbury-Barton. 'Why, I do believe it's John and Susan, and grown so much I should hardly have known them.'

The children shook hands and said they were very

well thank-you and agreed that it was nice to be back in Scatterbrook.

'Do you remember,' said Susan, when at last Mrs Bloomsbury-Barton had bustled away, 'Do you remember the time when she mistook Gummidge for a tramp and he asked her to change places with him?'

'Yes and then he pulled the feathers out of her hat.' John gave Mrs Kibbins' cat a farewell tickle under the chin before following Susan down the road.

They decided to go up to Ten-acre Field – the place where they had first met Worzel Gummidge.

The winding lane that led to it seemed shorter than it had done in Spring, perhaps because their legs were longer and perhaps because the cart ruts had dried and there was no mud to make their shoes heavy.

'Oh! if only he'll be here,' said Susan, as they reached the gate leading into Ten-acre Field.

The gate was topped with brushwood, its latch was awkward and it was so heavy that when at last it swung before them on its rusty hinges the children were both out of breath.

But they were not too breathless to gasp with disappointment, for the whole of the ten acres which had been brown in early spring was now golden with waist-high wheat.

'He'd never be here,' said Susan. 'They'd never let him stay here. Oh! what is that?'

'I don't see anything,' said John, staring beyond Susan's pointing finger to some scarlet poppies, and beyond them to a clump of scabious.

It really wasn't surprising that John could not see the old-fashioned sailor hat to which Susan was pointing. It was made of straw and it was sunburned to almost the exact colour of the wheat. The blue ribbon round the crown was faded so that it was nearly as pale as the scabious that nodded against the edge of the brim. The hat was moving slowly towards them, and at last John saw it.

'Gummidge!' he said. 'Worzel Gummidge, of course.'

'Don't be silly. Gummidge always wore a black bowler hat,' Susan reminded him. 'And Gummidge was tall – much taller than we are.'

'I told you scarecrows might shorten,' said John.

Suddenly the hat disappeared altogether, but the children could see that something was stirring in the wheat. Someone was breathing heavily, and someone was muttering in a rather unhappy sort of way. And then, as the muttering grew louder, the wheat rippled quite violently and the poppies waved though there was scarcely a breath of wind.

The wheat parted, and a very tiny creature whose sailor hat nearly covered its face staggered towards John and Susan. It was wearing a child's blue smock which came right down to what Susan guessed were its feet. Actually these were the flappy ends of fly swatters and the handles made its short and very thin legs. It had fly swatters for hands and arms too, and as soon as it was clear of the wheat it clapped these together, muttering, 'It's too bad – that it is!'

The voice was so plaintive that Susan went down on her knees and straightened the poor little thing's hat.

'What is too bad?' she asked gently.

The tiny scarecrow raised a red and extraordinarily muddy face. It was red because it had been carved out of a beetroot, and muddy because whoever had made the scarecrow had not been particular about washing. Susan did her best with a handkerchief, and soon she was able to make out several features quite clearly. The nose was a knobble; and a crack in the beetroot made quite a large mouth. It had two slits for eyes, and if one of these had not been so much higher than the other, it would, for a scarecrow, have been quite good looking.

Susan rubbed the flushed cheeks and repeated her question –

'What is too bad?'

'I've lost his hairbrush,' came the dismal answer.

'Whose hairbrush?' asked John.

'My uncle's, my Uncle Worzel's hairbrush.'

John and Susan both asked the same question at the same time.

'Do you mean Worzel Gummidge?'

They were almost afraid to hear the answer because they were so very much afraid that the small scarecrow's uncle might be Worzel something else. It did seem very unlikely that Worzel Gummidge would ever use a brush on his green sprouting tufts of hair.

As a matter of fact, there *was* no answer – at least not for some time. The little scarecrow puckered its mouth and clapped both its hands to the sides of its head.

'Oh dear' cried Susan. 'Have you got ear-ache?'

The scarecrow jerked its head forward then sideways and then forward again.

Susan was so afraid it would pull its head off that she took both the queer hands in her own, but they were wrenched away from her as John asked again, 'Is Worzel Gummidge your Uncle?'

Once more the head was jerked forward: this time more than once.

'I believe it's trying to nod,' said John.

'A'course I am,' said the creature. 'None of us but Uncle Worzel Gummidge has a hairbrush and now I've lost it.'

The poor little thing sounded so dismal and its face turned such a much brighter red that Susan, afraid it might be going to cry, said, 'We'll help you to look for it. Had the hairbrush a handle?'

'They don't have no handles,' sighed the scarecrow. 'All bristles and legs this one were.'

'Legs!' exclaimed John.

Once more the creature tried to make its peculiar nod.

'I'd not so much as turned my back a minute to scare a wasp when it were off.'

'The wasp, do you mean?' asked Susan patiently.

'The hairbrush!' screamed the scarecrow, and stamped a flapping foot. 'They run so fast there's no keeping up with 'em.'

It was all very puzzling, so puzzling that Susan and John looked at one another in despair. The scarecrow was still flapping its feet in an angry sort of way and its face was redder than ever. Susan, who had once seen a child behave like this before it went into a screaming fit, thought she had better change the subject.

'What is your name?' she asked.

'It's writ on my hat.'

The children stooped down and read the faded gold lettering on the hat-ribbon.

'H.M.S. Odney,' spelled John. 'I think it must have been H.M.S. Rodney before the R was washed out.'

'Listen,' said the scarecrow, 'That'll be it. There it is.'

It flapped a hand towards the edge of the cornfield.

There was a little rustling sound and slowly, very slowly, black nose followed by brown bristles, a small creature pushed its way out of the wheat.

'A hedgehog!' said John.

'His hairbrush,' said the scarecrow, as he flapped his way towards it.

At the very first touch of the fly-swatter foot, the hedgehog stopped and rolled itself into a ball.

John went and picked it up. He knew that if a hedgehog is handled gently its prickles do not hurt, so he rolled it over, touched the black nose that was so like a boot button and stroked the fur underneath.

'You're not to use it,' stormed the little scarecrow. 'My Uncle Worzel he won't share his hairbrush not with nobody not since he lent it to a friend and the bristles got all stuck up with tar.'

'John hasn't got any tar in his hair,' said Susan rather indignantly.

'It might be tar or it might be treacle,' said the little creature, 'there's never any telling. Gimme the hairbrush!' It folded its fly-swatter hands under the hem of the blue smock so as to make a sort of hammock. Then it looked up so pleadingly that John let it have the hedgehog.

'Where is Gummidge, I mean your Uncle Worzel?' asked Susan.

'He'll be up at the school, I expect.'

'Do you mean the school in the village?' asked John.

'I mean his school,' answered the red-faced scarecrow, and, turning its back on them, it moved flappingly down the lane. It was a slow walker because it kept treading on its own feet. John and Susan followed: they supposed it was going to return the hedgehog to Worzel Gummidge.

'Would you like us to carry you?' asked Susan, who thought that at this rate they would take at least an hour to reach the village.

The little scarecrow flopped one foot down on to the other one, swayed a little, and answered, 'I've never left the ground yet, nor I never will.'

'If you tell us where your Uncle Worzel is, we'll take the hedgehog, I mean the hairbrush to him,' suggested John, who was even more anxious than Susan to see Worzel Gummidge as soon as possible.

'I tells you I don't know where he is,' was the answer.
'I don't know where the school is.'

'Then where are you going?'

'Back to the allotment gardens where I belongs to.
My Uncle Worzel, he knows where to find me and when
he wants the hairbrush he'll come and fetch it.'

Susan longed to separate its feet because she was
afraid it might topple over, but she did not want to risk
annoying it, so she asked, 'When do you think he will
want the hairbrush?'

'Might be to-day, might be to-morrow, might be next
week or not till corn-harvest. And I can't stand here
talking. I've got to get back.'

'Then let's talk as we walk along, shall we?'

Susan spoke in her most soothing voice, but the
scarecrow answered quite crossly –

'I can't work my mouth *and* my legs at the same time,
can I?'

'Can't you?' said John.

'I'll show you I can't,' replied the queer little scarecrow. Then it lifted one foot, put the other on top of it,
and went on repeating this curious exercise.

Susan coaxed and John scolded, but it did not say
another word and after five minutes had gone by and
about one yard had been travelled, they looked despairingly at one another and ran on ahead.

'I don't believe Gummidge *can* be in the school,' said
Susan. 'It's shut up now for the holidays. Oh! look!'

They had reached a gateway, and Susan began to
point in an excited sort of way.

'I don't see anything,' said John.

Then a puff of wind blew Susan's hair forward and
went on its way to flutter a label that was tied to the
top of a gate-post. Susan ran towards it, and John
stared as she snatched at the dancing label.

' "This side up with care",' she read. 'Oh! what a pity!'

'I don't see that it's a pity. What did you expect to find?'

'I thought there might be a message from Gummidge ... Wait a bit ... there *is* something written on the other side and it's in awfully Gummidgy writing ... I should think he used a bit of coal.'

'What does it say?' asked John impatiently.

For answer, Susan spread out the label. There in writing that was thick in some places, thin in others and smudged all over were the words –

'TuRnEPS BACK o BARNe, W. GuM.'

'What does it mean, do you think?' asked John.

'I suppose it means that Gummidge is eating turnips at the back of the barn.'

'I don't think he'd *eat* turnips,' John's voice was thoughtful. 'I don't *think* he'd eat turnips considering that his head is made out of a turnip. I don't think he's a cannibal. But we'd better go and see.'

CHAPTER II

A SCHOOL FOR SCARECROWS

—

So they went to see, but they had to leave the Downs before they found a barn standing at the edge of a field of roots.

'Listen!' said Susan, 'there's somebody talking inside.' But there was nobody in the barn – nothing at all, in fact, except a heap of straw in a corner and a rusty turnip-chopper in the middle. All the same, the voice went on and the children stood quite still to listen.

'It's Gummidge's voice,' whispered Susan. 'I know

it's –' Before she could finish her sentence, the voice ended in a husky sort of cough.

'Gummidge's cough!' cried John, 'and I think he's saying poetry.'

The voice went on in a creaky monotonous way that reminded the children of the sound of an old pump. Not that they had ever heard a pump repeating even *queer* poetry.

> *'One rook's same as t'other –*
> *If it isn't ask your mother.*
>
> *Two rooks never matter.*
> *Three rooks is much more fatter.*
>
> *Six rooks'll make their double.*
> *Eight rooks means lots o' trouble.*
>
> *Ten rooks is past all bearing.*
> *Twelve rooks means scarecrows scaring.*
> *Flap! FLAP! FLAP! FLAP! FLAP!'*

'Whatever can he be doing?' asked Susan, and then she and John tiptoed to the wall of the barn and peeped through a crevice between two chinks of wood and into the turnip field.

There with his back to them sat Worzel Gummidge, the scarecrow of Scatterbrook. They knew him at once by the way his broom-stick arms stuck straight out from the shoulders and showed an inch or two of polished wrist between the tattered cuffs of his coat sleeves and his twig-like fingers. His bowler hat was perched sideways on his turnipy head. He was wearing an old check duster as a scarf.

'Gummidge!' said Susan.

'Flap! Flap! Flap! Flap! Flap!' repeated the scarecrow, moving his arms up and down rather in the way that a hawk quivers its wings just before swooping. 'Flap! Flap! Flap!' A light wind fluttered his sleeves and then went on to ruffle the leaves of the turnips.

'Gummidge!' said John.

'You can go on learning by yourselves,' shouted Gummidge to no one that the children could see. Then he jerked himself upright and came shuffling towards them on his broomstick legs. He was still wearing his old bottle-straw boots. His coat was open and a few strands of tarred string crossed his faded blue shirt. These, they remembered, were his braces.

They were glad to see that his face had not changed at all. It was still turnipy, and just now it was creased into pleasant wrinkles. A few green sprouts showed below the bowler hat and his nose was as knobbly as ever.

'How are you?' asked Susan and John both at the same time.

'Quite well in places,' answered Gummidge, and he paused to stuff back a tuft of hay which was showing between the buttons of his shirt. My legs is all right and my head's all right, but the sparrows have been trying to steal my stummick again. Why can't they get their own hay for their own nests – that's what I tells 'em.'

'Poor Gummidge!' said Susan.

'We've come back to Scatterbrook for part of the holidays,' added John.

'Ooh aye! I heard that this arternoon,' said Gummidge.

'How did you hear?'

'Gossip gets about,' said the scarecrow carelessly. 'If you *wants* to know I heard it from one of the station pigeons. In a fair tantrum she were, when she flew over to tell me the news. I've never heard a bird say so many nasty things between two mouthfuls. Cruel she said you were.'

'But we've never hurt one of the station pigeons,' said John rather indignantly.

'Not hurt them may be,' said Gummidge, 'but you'd get peevish yourself if you had your dinner trod on.'

'Dinner trod on?' repeated Susan.

'I said dinner trod on and I meant dinner trod on, leastways I meant a snack before meals trod on. There was a passenger parrot that had been throwing its seed about and you went and trod on it afore the pigeon had time to peck. Leastways, that's what she told me.'

'I'm very sorry,' said Susan.

'Ooh aye! So you did ought to be. And so you did ought to be sorry for interruptin' my class. I'm that busy I don't know what to do. Eddicatin' scarecrows – that's what I'm doing.'

John and Susan glanced round the field, but all they could see were rows and rows of turnips, and here and there a spider's web shimmering among the dark leaves. There was no sign of a scarecrow and Susan said so.

'Not yet there isn't,' agreed Gummidge, 'but there's no tellin' which of 'em may be scarecrows.'

'Which of who?' asked John.

Gummidge waved an arm creakily in the direction of the turnips. Then he turned back towards the edge of the field and sat down with a bump, his legs sticking straight out in front of him. The children sat down one on each side of him, and John repeated the question.

'Anyone that's got any sense,' said Gummidge, 'Anyone that's got a *bit* of sense knows that all the best scarecrow's heads is made out of turnips same as mine is. I've got a nice class here – a whole field o' fine turnips, and when I've done with eddicatin' them they'll be all ready to fend for theirselves by the time they've had their bodies made.'

'It seems a funny way of doing it,' said Susan. 'I

mean it seems queer to educate heads that haven't got any bodies.'

Gummidge picked up a lump of chalk and flung it at a turnip whose green leaves were fluttering in the wind.

'Give over rustling,' he ordered. Then he turned to Susan and said "Taint queer at all: it's the proper way of doin' things. Folks don't learn with their bodies; they learns in their heads.'

'But when we're at school –' began John.

Gummidge interrupted him quite crossly. 'When you're at school, you're wearin' out your arms and legs. Ooh aye, and growin' out of your clothes too, and putting food into your mouths and taking up a lot more room than your heads need. Downright wasteful, I calls it. But your sort never did have no sense. Daft, that's what you are – all the lot of you.'

'We aren't all daft,' said Susan, and John added, 'Our old governess used to say that we ought to have sane minds in sound bodies.'

'Then that shows she was daft. Everybody knows minds don't grow in bodies – they grows in heads. I've never known but one daft scarecrow, and she'd had a lump cut out of her head with a turnip slicer when her and another she-scarecrow was cutting each other's hair. Quite daft she were after that, poor thing. Many's the time I've heard her talking to the moon afore it got to the full. "You and me ought to get married," she says to him. "You and me'd get on fine together. We've both been sufferers – we've both lost bits out of our head," she says. Ooh aye – she were happy enough when the moon was at the three-quarters, but when it was at the full she sobbed something pitiful.'

'Why?' asked Susan.

Gummidge looked at her rather contemptuously. 'She thought he'd been mended, or grown a new

side to his head, and she kept on saying it wasn't fair
that he should be cured and she not.'

'What did she think about the new moon?' asked John.

'That were the only time she were cheerful – to
think that he were worse off nor she. She'll be abroad
now, I daresay. Me and Earthy helped her to stow
herself away in an aeroplane. It had landed on the
Downs and she thought it would be going to the moon
most like. But I can't sit chattering all day. I've got to
get on with the class now. I've finished the 'rithmetic.
We did the History yesterday and we'll have to get on
with the Geography now. I'll start with the front row first.'

Worzel Gummidge jerked himself upright and
shuffled sideways towards the front row of the turnips.
Then he seized two of them firmly by the tops and began
to pull.

John and Susan were surprised to see that the turnips
really had got faces. One of them looked as if it was
squinting. The other had a lop-sided mouth and a
knobble that was in the right place for a nose even if it
wasn't very shapely.

'What are you doing?' asked Susan as Gummidge
continued to wrench at the turnip-tops.

'Geography!' he answered, and just as he spoke two
of the turnips came up so suddenly that he nearly sat
down again. He gave them an impatient shake and
began to shuffle across the field towards an empty farm-
cart that was resting on its shafts quite near the barn.
Into the cart went the turnips, and Worzel Gummidge
returned to the front row for another couple.

'I thought you said you were going to do Geography?'
said John.

'So I am doing Geography.' Gummidge gave the
next pair of turnips a shake. 'Geography means places
– not one place – it means places that folk goes to and

all about 'em. That's why I'm taking the turnips somewhere else. 'Tis only sense.'

'That's not the way we learn Geography.'

'It's the way I teaches it!' snapped Gummidge. 'And
if you keep on interfering I'll sulk. You can help if you
like.'

But John and Susan didn't feel inclined to help. They
weren't at all sure what Farmer Braithewaite would say
if he knew that so many of his turnips were being
dragged up and pitched into the farm cart, but they did
know that it was not a bit of good interfering with Worzel
Gummidge when he was in an obstinate mood.

So they sat and watched while the scarecrow shambled
backwards and forwards.

'I really don't think you ought to do that,' said Susan,
as Gummidge shuffled by with two particularly fierce-
looking turnips from the second row.

'And I thinks I ought,' he grunted. 'Scarecrows has got
to learn Jography – else they'll never find their way about.'

'Geography,' replied Susan primly, 'Geography is
learning about foreign places, and towns – and – mountains and – and rivers and things like that, you know.'

Gummidge swung the two fierce turnips so savagely
that Susan was afraid he would wrench their tops off.

'Depends where you are,' he said slowly. 'There
aren't no foreign places nor mountains nor towns in
Scatterbrook and there ain't no river neither. There's
only the brook.' He added obligingly. 'You can chuck
'em in the brook if you like.'

To Susan's surprise he dropped the two turnips on
to her lap. They were very heavy, and they covered her
frock with earth.

'I don't want to throw them into the brook,' she said,
glancing down at the two angry faces of the turnips as
they lay glaring up at her.

'You've drove me to it,' said Gummidge, 'You and your interferin' ways. I'm going to have a real good sulk.'

He sat down so suddenly that he was almost hidden for a moment by a little cloud of dust. Some of it got into the children's eyes, and by the time they had wiped these clear again, he had fallen into one of his very worst sulks. His face now looked even more like a turnip than the two roots that lay on Susan's lap. He was breathing angrily, and as he breathed they could hear the rustling of his straw stuffing. Every second he was growing more and more like the sort of scarecrow that nobody would believe could ever possibly come to life.

'Gummidge,' pleaded Susan, and she laid her hand on one of his stiff broomstick arms. 'Please, please don't sulk the very first day we've come back to Scatterbrook.'

There was no answer, and so John tried.

'Aren't you *pleased* to see us, Gummidge?' he asked.

Worzel Gummidge closed his eyes so tightly that only two very thin slits showed on either side of the knobble that was his nose.

'I *can't* see you,' he said quite truthfully. Then he let himself go from the waist like a flap door with weak hinges, and lay back on the ground with a creak and a rustle.

John and Susan sat there for some time, because they hoped he might stop sulking. They had learned in the Spring that he had a habit of falling into a deep sulk whenever he was annoyed. They were not frightened, but they were very disappointed.

'We'd better go back, I should think,' said John, after he had prodded Gummidge in the middle and received no answer but a rustle. 'He may sulk for days.'

'Or weeks,' said Susan sadly. 'I wonder what we'd better do with these?'

'Put them in the cart, I should think.'

'P'raps we'd better ask them first,' said Susan, because the turnips had such annoyed-looking faces.

But evidently they had not learned to speak yet, even though they were the pupils of Gummidge's strange school. Their expressions did not change at all when Susan asked, 'Please, do you mind if I get up now?'

'They're awfully ugly, aren't they?' said John.

'Hush!' Susan stroked the muddy faces gently because she was so afraid that they might not be deaf even though they had not yet learned to speak. 'Don't hurt their feelings.'

Then she gave one to John, picked up the other herself, dusted her frock and walked towards the cart.

'Hi!' said a voice from the gateway. 'What do you think you're doing?'

It was Farmer Braithewaite and he was leading Biddy, the old mare, because the cart was needed down at the farm.

'I was –' said Susan, and she put the turnip into the cart with some of its schoolfellows.

'I was just putting this into the cart,' said John, as the other followed.

Farmer Braithewaite dropped Biddy's bridle and looked into the cart.

'This is a good beginning,' he said. 'Yes, this is a nice beginning to a holiday. Why did you want to go pulling up my turnips before they're ready?'

'We – we didn't,' said Susan.

'Now don't tell me that when I saw you putting them into the cart.'

'I mean, I mean we didn't *want* to pull them up and – and Oh! dear!'

Susan looked appealing at the sulking scarecrow. Two or three wasps were crawling about his face, and she felt that if anything could make him speak they would, but Gummidge never stirred.

Perhaps the miserable note in her voice made the farmer feel sorry for having spoken crossly.

'Well, there isn't so much harm done,' he said. 'But next time you want to help on the farm ask me first.' As he spoke he began to harness Biddy to the cart. 'You'd best drive back with me,' he said. 'Steady now, lass.' The last remark was made to Biddy.

It was not until they were driving out of the field that the farmer noticed Worzel Gummidge. With a 'whoa then!' to Biddy, he jumped down from the cart.

'That old scarecrow's an untidy sight,' he said. 'I'll take it back to the farm. Mrs Braithewaite may like to cut up his coat into shreds for one of her rag carpets.'

He picked Gummidge up and dumped him into the cart on to the top of the turnips.

'Yes, we'll use his coat for shreds,' he repeated. 'We're always short of them. If the coat's not good enough for rug-making it will do for shreds for nailing up the fruit-trees. Now that's a job you *can* do.'

'Nailing up the fruit-trees?' asked John hopefully.

'No, cut up the coat into shreds,' was the dreadful answer. 'It will keep you out of mischief.'

Susan looked at John, John looked at Susan and they both looked at Worzel Gummidge, who gave no sign of having heard a word. His head joggled gently against the other turnips as Biddy pulled the cart into the lane.

Mrs Braithewaite was feeding the chickens when the farmer drove Biddy into the yard. She looked up and waved to them and just then John sneezed. It was a loud sneeze, and only meant that a tiny bit of feather or dust had tickled his nose, but Mrs Braithewaite, who was dreadfully fussy about colds and things, looked up sharply.

'Now then,' she said, 'who's caught a cold?'

For answer, John sneezed again. He was sitting with his back to the farmer's wife, but she saw the shake of his shoulders and before he could explain that it was only a tickle and not a cold, another enormously loud sneeze made him jump. The sneeze was followed by another and another and another. Worzel Gummidge the scarecrow was being tiresome again.

Neither John nor Susan had known before that he could sneeze, though they had often heard him cough. The farmer had his back to the cart and could not see the extraordinary faces that the scarecrow was making; nor could Mrs Braithewaite because she was standing on the ground.

'Hay fever!' she said, 'I know hay fever when I hear it. There'll be no more running about in the fields for a day or two, I can tell you *that*.'

'It was only a tickle,' explained John, as he jumped down from the cart and Susan followed him.

Then most unfortunately Gummidge sneezed again.

'Hay fever!' repeated Mrs Braithewaite. 'Into the house with you both.'

'And while they're in the house there's something to keep them amused,' said the farmer, and he heaved Gummidge out of the cart.

'Why! If it's not the old scarecrow you used to set up in Ten-acre Field. You're never going to let them have *that* to play with, littering up the place with straw.'

'That I'm not,' agreed the farmer. 'I'll throw it up into the loft until we want it next spring.'

'We'll take him up to the loft,' said Susan.

'Yes, we'll take him,' echoed John.

'That you won't with hay fever.' Mrs Braithewaite's voice was very firm. 'Lofts and hay-fields are the worst places of all for that.'

'I haven't –' began John, but the farmer interrupted by explaining that he wanted the children to cut up Gummidge's coat for garden shreds.

There was nothing for them to do but to stand miserably by while the farmer jerked at Gummidge's coat, tugging the broomstick arms from the coat-sleeves and making the straw stuffing rustle. There lay the scarecrow still in a dead sulk, his broomstick arms sticking out absurdly from the sleeves of his faded blue shirt, his hat over his face and his tarred string braces looking more untidy than ever.

'He hasn't changed a bit,' whispered Susan, as the farmer threw Gummidge over his shoulder and tramped off towards the loft.

Five minutes later they were sitting dismally in the old dairy with Gummidge's coat between them and a pair of scissors each.

'If we say we won't, she'll only give the coat to somebody else,' said Susan. 'And perhaps if we cut very slowly we may be able to save a bit for Gummidge.'

They did cut slowly; Mrs Braithewaite said so when she returned to the dairy and Susan held up the coat which had had one-and-a-half-inch strips cut from all round the bottom and from the ends of the cuffs. Each strip was an inch apart, and so the coat looked as if it had been fringed. She hung it on a lavender bush outside, gathered the shreds together and told the children that it was time for supper.

It was too hot to go to bed very early that night so Susan and John (because, after all, he had not sneezed again) were allowed to go and sit on the wall that divided the flower-garden from a little paddock. The farmer had told them that they would see the moon rise there. It was very still, so still that they only liked to talk in whispers for fear of disturbing birds and other small night creatures that had gone to bed. A mixture of scent rose up from the sweet jumble of flowers at the foot of the wall – cherry-pie, sweet briar and the night scented stock that always reminded Susan of tiny butterflies.

The moon rose slowly and in such a fiery glow that they wondered for a minute or two whether the sun had made a mistake and was getting up at the wrong time. Then just as its very lowest edge seemed to be clear of the Downs, they noticed two figures climbing in a lumbering way over the opposite wall of the paddock.

'I wonder who they are?' said Susan.

'Ladies, I think,' said John.

A sheep-like cough startled him and a husky voice agreed –

'Ooh aye! O' course, they're ladies. That'll be Earthy and Hannah. You can tell by the way they walks.'

The voice belonged to Gummidge, of course. Somehow or other he had got out of the loft. His bottle-straw boots moved almost silently through the soft grass so they had not heard him.

Nearer and nearer came the two quaint figures. The shorter one moved hoppingly like a robin and the taller one had an unhappy shambling way of moving her feet.

John and Susan ran to meet them while Worzel Gummidge shuffled after them.

It was nice to feel the twiggy fingers of Earthy Mangold, Gummidge's pleasant little wife, and when she lifted up her face, Susan stooped down and kissed her. She never had kissed a scarecrow before, and it was a rather queer experience. Earthy's face was damp with dew and her cheek smelled of freshly-dug potatoes and parsley. Susan could feel the roughness of her sacking cloak, and she hoped that Earthy was still wearing her blue-and-white checked apron.

'Evening, my dear,' said Earthy. 'Nobody but Worzel's ever kissed me before.'

'*Nobody's* never kissed me,' said Hannah Harrow plaintively. Susan felt so sorry for the dismal scarecrow that she did try to kiss her, but though she stood on tip-toe, she could not reach her face, and Hannah did not seem to understand about stooping. Susan was rather glad really, because though she could not see Hannah's face, she remembered that it had always looked dingy, and she could smell the tarred string that the scarecrow had instead of hair.

'Welcome to Scatterbrook,' said Hannah. Earthy added –

'One of the bats from the barn told us you'd come.'

'Gossiping creature!' said Hannah. 'Mice is bad enough when they keep on nibbling at your stuffing, but mice don't go whirling about in the air. I've always been a cruel sufferer from the mice, but I've not had the bats yet.'

'Where are you –?' began Susan, but just then Mrs Braithewaite's voice interrupted. She was calling to them through the open window to hurry up and come to bed.

'We'd best be getting along then too,' said Earthy. 'Come and see us to-morrow.'

'John! Susan!' repeated Mrs Braithewaite, and because they could hear the sound of a door being opened, the children turned and ran quickly across the grass. They were afraid that Mrs Braithewaite might come into the garden and see their friends.

When they had climbed the wall again, they turned back to look at Earthy, Hannah, and Gummidge who were hopping, trailing, and shambling away from them.

'And we never had a chance to ask where they all live now,' sighed Susan.

CHAPTER III

GUMMIDGE'S HOME

—

THE next morning Mrs Braithewaite had news for them. There was, she said, to be a Garden Fête in the village of Penfold which was a mile away from Scatterbrook, and she thought that the children would like to go. John and Susan were not so sure about this because Fêtes generally mean best uncomfortable clothes – nails sore from sharp cleaning, heads aching after the hair-brush and faces smelling of soaped flannel. But when Mrs Braithewaite added that there was to be a parade for boys and girls under the age of fifteen with prizes for the prettiest and the most original fancy dresses they rather changed their minds.

Mrs Braithewaite suggested that Susan should go as Miss Muffet in a mob-cap and a long sticking-out frock, mittens and a spotted muslin apron, and that John should go as Little Tommy Tucker. She said she could easily make him a frilly collar.

That sounded a perfectly horrid idea to John and he might have said so if it hadn't been for Susan's sudden idea.

'Let's go as scarecrows,' she said, 'scarecrows with bottle-straw boots and raggedy clothes. Oh! do let us, *please*. We can dress ourselves up and you needn't bother a bit.'

'Scarecrows?' repeated Mrs Braithewaite, 'Scarecrows, you've got scarecrows on the brain. All right, go as scarecrows if you want to.'

After that John and Susan were in such a hurry to finish breakfast that they didn't even bother to write their names in golden syrup on their porridge.

As soon as breakfast was over they had a dress rehearsal. John rubbed his face all over with crushed walnut leaves until it was a streaky brown. He turned his oldest pair of flannel trousers inside out, and put a broomstick handle through the sleeves of Gummidge's coat which he had taken from the lavender bush outside the old dairy. Luckily the coat was much too big, so he knew that even after he had padded himself out with hay he would be able to keep his own arms out of sight and hanging down quite comfortably. There was a very old bowler hat in the barn, and this was quite a good fit after it had been padded out with hay.

Susan used walnut leaves and blackberry juice for her face. She tied a bit of sacking round her waist for a skirt, turned another bit of sacking into a cloak, borrowed a check apron from Mrs Braithewaite, stuffed some brown woollen gloves with paper and twisted a fish bass into something that didn't look quite like either a hat or a sun-bonnet.

After the children had both finished dressing-up, they pulled bottle-straws over their shoes and went out to practise walking like scarecrows.

Susan went hoppingly like Earthy Mangold, John went crabwise in the way that Worzel Gummidge walked; so it took them rather a long time even to get out of the farm-yard.

'I wish we could find out where *they* live,' said Susan, stopping to put on her bottle-straws again for the fourth time; 'I mean, I wish we could find out where Gummidge and Earthy live so that we could call on them.'

'Yes,' agreed John; 'but they might be anywhere. They might be nesting – we know Gummidge likes

nests – or they may have made a sort of dug-out or
burrow or something; he always looks muddy.'

Susan took two or three more hops, lost another bottle-
straw overshoe, put it on again and said:

'Let's go to the Allotment Gardens, and see if we can
find that funny little scarecrow, H.M.S. Odney, the one
who was keeping the hedgehog. P'raps he'll know where
Gummidge is.'

So they took off the straw overshoes and hurried to the
Allotment Gardens by a roundabout way because they
did not want to meet anybody.

No one was working in the allotments, so they walked
across a plot of ground to where the tiny scarecrow was
standing surrounded by cabbages. Its face looked redder
than ever and there were two or three pink tears on its
cheeks. Susan noticed at once that there was something
wrong with it, something missing, but just at first she
could not think what.

'Why,' said John suddenly, 'what has happened to
your arms?'

'They're being used,' answered the little creature
sadly; and added, 'I can't shake hands.'

Of course it could not shake hands because both hands
and arms had gone. Susan looked down anxiously, but
the fly-swatter feet were still in place and little scraps of
cabbage leaves caught in their meshes.

'You poor little thing!' she said.

The small scarecrow flapped a foot.

'Not poor!' it shouted. 'I've two stamps in my pocket.
Look! Take 'em out. Look!'

Susan felt in the patch-pocket of its smock, and pulled
out two envelopes. They were very dirty and each one
had a used halfpenny stamp.

'Penny!' said the scarecrow proudly. 'Put 'em back.'

Susan had not the heart to tell it that the stamps were

worth nothing, so she asked, 'How did you lose your arms?'

'Mrs Kibbins took 'em. This here's her allotment. She's making jam to-day, so she's got a lot of wasps to swat. She often takes 'em, but she'll put 'em back to-night.'

'So that's all right, isn't it?' said Susan.

'Not all right. Uncle Worzel wants his hairbrush most partickler, and it keeps getting away from under my feet. There it goes again!'

The hedgehog pushed its way between two cabbage stalks and scurried on until John made a grab at it.

'We'll take it,' said Susan, 'if you'll tell us where Gummidge is.'

'They're caravanning now,' said the creature, 'you'll find 'em up in the old van by the lambing pens. I'm going to have my arternoon sleep now, same as I always does. Good arternoon.'

The abrupt ways of the small scarecrow showed that it must be some relation of Worzel Gummidge's. As soon as it had finished speaking, it turned its back slowly.

'Shall I help you to lie down?' asked Susan. 'You may find it rather difficult now that your arms have gone.'

There was no answer, and Susan, remembering that it was rather a touchy little creature, added, 'unless, of course, you're used to it.'

There was still no answer, so she tiptoed round to the front. The scarecrow's pink tears had dried by now, its eyes were tightly shut. Evidently it had gone to sleep on its feet, in much the same way that Worzel Gummidge fell into sulks.

'Do come on,' begged John, who was holding the hedgehog with a good deal of difficulty because he could only get his arms a little way through the gaps between his coat-buttons.

Susan made a hammock of her apron for the hedgehog and then they hurried off towards the fold in the Downs where the old caravan stood.

Worzel Gummidge was sitting on the little ladder that led up to its door. As soon as he saw them he got up and began to wave his arms.

'Go away!' he shouted. 'We don't want no more scarecrows.'

'It's only us,' said John.

'It's a great deal too bad. Ooh aye! it's a great deal more than a great deal too bad. Turning yourselves into scarecrows and trying to take the food out of other scarecrows' mouths.'

Susan glanced at Gummidge's muddy mouth and gave a little shudder.

'We wouldn't do that, really we wouldn't,' she said. 'We wouldn't *like* to.'

Gummidge looked at her in a disbelieving sort of way, and Susan, thinking that he might be pleased to see the hedgehog, rolled it out of her apron.

'Go and find your own hairbrushes,' said Gummidge angrily, 'and don't go using mine.'

'We were only bringing it back to you,' said Susan.

'A likely story when it's got legs of its own.' Gummidge jerked himself on to the grass and the hedgehog scurried up to him and began to rub its bristles against the straw of Gummidge's boots.

'It does shoe-cleaning and all sorts,' he remarked proudly. 'Worth its weight in turnips that hairbrush is.'

As Gummidge seemed to be in a slightly better temper, John and Susan told him about the fête at Penfold and why they had dressed up as scarecrows.

'We shan't go on being scarecrows after to-day,' she added.

'You'll not be able to stop yourselves,' said Gummidge gloomily, 'no more than chickens can stop being chickens

once they've started. They never turns back into eggs
again.'

'Of course they don't,' said John; 'they turn into cocks
and hens.'

'Just as John will turn into a man and I shall turn into
a woman,' explained Susan.

'No, you won't – not now.' Gummidge sounded so
absolutely certain of this that the children began to
feel a little worried, and Susan even began to pinch one
of her arms to make sure it had not turned into wood;
while John touched his face nervously to feel if it was at
all turnipy.

'I'll tell you for why that you won't,' went on Gummidge, 'it's a grand life a scarecrow's is. Ooh aye, it's a
grand life. We stops where we likes and we goes where
we likes.'

'So do people,' said John.

'People don't take to bits,' said Gummidge, 'that
makes all the difference.'

As they could not think of any answer to this, John and
Susan watched in silence while Gummidge took off his
hat, picked up the hedgehog, and began to brush the
tufts of his green and sprouting hair.

'The best part of this sort of brush,' he said, 'the very
best part of this sort of brush is that if you happens to get
slugs or blackbeetles in the hair, the brush will eat them.
I'll lend it you one day and then you'll see.'

Susan shuddered, and John said indignantly:

'We never never have blackbeetles *or* slugs in our hair.'

'You will now you've turned into scarecrows.' Gummidge put down the hedgehog and watched it crawl
away under the caravan. 'Leastwise you will if you sleeps
in the same place for long enough. Ants too.'

Once more the children tried to explain to Gummidge
that they had not really turned into scarecrows, but as

they could not make him understand, Susan asked if
Earthy was inside the caravan.

'Ooh aye! She's there and so's Hannah, but they're
not talking to-day because of their veils.'

'What do you mean?' asked Susan.

Instead of answering, Worzel Gummidge got up and
walked sideways towards the caravan. He put out a stiff
arm and pushed at the door which swung open creakily.
John and Susan followed him inside.

Earthy Mangold was sitting on the floor and beside
her sat Hannah Harrow. Each had a large spider on the
tip of her nose.

As soon as she saw them, Susan understood what
Worzel Gummidge had meant about their veils. For the
two spiders had spun two beautiful cart-wheel veils
right across their faces. Silvery threads were entwined
with Hannah Harrow's tarred-string hair and among
the little green tufts which sprouted low down on Earthy
Mangold's forehead. John and Susan had never noticed
before that Gummidge's wife had eyebrows. True one
was higher than the other, but they were both quite
shapely and contrasted well with the brown of her
potato-like face.

'Now, don't you talk,' said Gummidge to his wife and
to Hannah. 'They've only come to look.' He turned to
the children and added, 'It's lucky they've *both* got
veils. She-scarecrows do get that jealous of one another.
Smart, aren't they?'

Susan nodded. She was afraid that if she spoke she
might laugh because both Hannah and Earthy were
squinting violently at the spiders on their noses.

'Once on a time,' Gummidge told them. 'Once on a
time there were a she-scarecrow that was dressed all
over in spiders' veiling. They'd left her in a loft all
Summer and she were much too proud to move.'

'What happened to her?' asked Susan.

'I don't know what happened to her after what did happen,' said Gummidge.

'What *did* happen?' asked John.

'The farmer found her and swept all the clothes off of her with a broom,' answered Gummidge, 'leastwise he swept all the cobweb clothes off of her.'

'How dreadful,' said Susan.

'Ooh aye!' agreed Gummidge, 'How do you like our furniture?'

John and Susan looked round the caravan, but they could not see any furniture at all, not even a packing case or a piece of sacking. Two or three notices were hung up on the wall – 'Wet Paint' – 'Stick No Bills' – 'Bridle Path Only' and 'This Side Up With Care.'

'What do you think of the furniture?' repeated Gummidge crossly.

'These are very nice,' John pointed to the notices on the walls, and tried to make his voice sound as polite as possible.

'Ooh aye! We're all fond of readin',' agreed Gummidge. 'But how do you like the furniture?'

The children glanced despairingly round the van, then shuffled their feet and looked down at the floor. In the middle of it a circle had been drawn in white chalk and two or three squares had been marked out in blue and red chalk.

'That's the table,' said Gummidge, moving a strawboot towards the circle, 'and them's the chairs.' He walked over and sat down abruptly on one of the chalked squares.

'I don't see any chair,' said Susan.

Gummidge patted another of the chalked squares. 'This here's a chair,' he explained. 'Sit down, can't you.'

Susan sat down on the chalk and remarked, 'It isn't what I'd call a chair.'

'Don't matter what you call it. A chair's something

you sits on and you can sit on these chairs, can't you?'

'Y—yes, but –'

'And a table's what you sits round and you can sit round *that*, can't you?'

John looked doubtfully at the chalked circle and opened his mouth to argue, but Gummidge went on –

'Tables is used for putting things on and you can put things on that one. Chairs is no use except for sitting on.'

There was a pause, and then, as neither Gummidge, Earthy nor Hannah spoke, Susan got up.

'I think perhaps we'd better be going now,' she said.

'Then why don't you?' asked Gummidge.

There was really no answer to that question either, so John and Susan walked out of the caravan.

CHAPTER IV

CHANGING PLACES

—

THEY went to a field and there they practised their scarecrow walks until their legs ached, and their inside-clocks told them that it must be dinner-time.

When they reached the farm Mrs Braithewaite was looking very flustered.

'Why didn't you hurry back when Dick told you to?' she asked.

'We never saw Dick,' answered John.

'There's none so blind as those that won't see,' was Mrs Braithewaite's answer. 'Dick saw you anyway, when you were playing about near the old lambing-pens and he said you answered him.'

'But we –' began Susan, and then a kick from John stopped her from saying anything more.

'I suppose you'll say next,' said Mrs Braithewaite, as she hustled them into the kitchen, 'I suppose you'll say next that you didn't hear Dick telling you to hurry up because the fête at Penfold begins half an hour earlier than I thought it did.'

Luckily Mrs Braithewaite went on talking to herself and complaining about the tiresome ways of children, so there was no need for John and Susan to answer her questions. They guessed, of course, that Dick, the cow-man, must have given the message to Worzel Gummidge and Earthy. They wondered what had happened then, and quite soon they knew.

'Next time Dick brings a message from me, don't throw bits of turnip at him,' warned Mrs Braithewaite. 'It's not a thing well-behaved children do, even if they are pretending to be scarecrows.'

'It's not a thing scarecrows do either,' said Farmer Braithewaite; 'at least I've never met one that was so active.'

It was very hard not to be able to explain that they would never think of throwing turnips at Dick the cow-man, who was always so kind to them, but, as John said afterwards, it was rather exciting to think that scarecrows really had been mistaken for them.

The moment they had finished dinner, Farmer Braithewaite helped them into the dog-cart and drove them over to Penfold where he left them.

It felt queer and very exciting to be allowed to go to a garden fête with dirty hands and faces, and with hair that had been ruffled up on purpose.

'You know,' said John, as he and Susan passed a group of newly-washed children, looking dreadfully stiff and uncomfortable in party frocks and best suits; 'You know if it wasn't for having to wear a broomstick through my coat sleeves, I think I'd rather like to be a scarecrow for always.'

Just at first the fête was rather dull and tiresome because John and Susan were laughed at so often and stared at so much and told that they looked exactly like scarecrows. After a time, though, it began to be fun. It was John's idea that they should go and stand very very still in different parts of the garden so as to see if anybody would really mistake them for scarecrows. But though it was John's idea he had the worst of it when he planted himself in a dahlia bed. Two old gentlemen came past, and after they had looked at the flowers and had agreed that the ones they had at home were much finer and bigger, one of them said, 'Those scarecrows may not look very tidy but they make good ear-wig traps. Look!'

He lifted his cane and prodded John so hard in the middle that he said 'Ow!' and clutched himself and nearly bent double. By the time he had straightened up again the two old gentlemen were walking away and talking very determinedly about the British Empire because they were the sort of people who couldn't see jokes or believe in anything unlikely.

Susan had a much better time. Nobody touched her, but one old lady said to another that she had never seen such a well-made scarecrow and that it showed that farmers and gardeners took their work much more seriously now than they used to.

When John found her she was looking red in the face and quite fat through trying to keep back her laughter without bursting.

'I know now what the figures in Madame Tussaud's feel like when people talk about them,' she said.

John, who was still feeling rather tender in the middle, said crossly, 'The figures in Madame Tussaud's don't feel anything: they're only imitation people.'

'So are scarecrows, but they *feel*,' said Susan. 'I think the waxworks are all sort of Gummidges, and that they all come alive at night and have fun.'

'Rubbish!' said John.

Just then somebody on the lawn picked up a megaphone and asked all the competitors in the fancy-dress parade to join in a procession and walk past the judges.

A pierrot and a peasant marched in front of John and Susan. Behind them came a Darby and Joan.

John shuffled along sideways and Susan imitated the hopping walk of Earthy Mangold. Round and round the lawn they walked until they got tired of losing their bottle-straws and finding them again. At last the music stopped and the man with the megaphone announced – 'The prizes for the *prettiest* fancy dresses have been won by the Rainbow Fairy and Little Bo Peep. The prizes for the most *original* costumes have been won by the two Scarecrows. Prizes will be distributed at five o'clock.'

Everybody clapped a great deal, and John and Susan went behind some laurel bushes where they changed the straw-boots for their own shoes, and John took the broomstick out of his coat sleeves so that he could be free to play in the skittles competition.

The fête was very much like other fêtes. There were blackberries and cream for tea. There was an ice-cream stall, a fancy stall, a skittle alley, and a tent with a fortune-teller inside it.

There were so many things to do and see and eat that the children forgot all about the time until John suddenly pulled out his watch.

'Ten past five,' he said, 'and the prize-giving's at five. We'd better hurry.'

They did hurry, and when they reached the big lawn they guessed that the crowd of people who were all

standing with their backs to the gravel must be waiting
for the prize-giving to begin.

Then the sound of clapping told them that it had
probably begun already; and when the clapping stopped
the man with the megaphone told them the same thing
only much more distinctly.

'The prizes for the most original costumes go to the two
scarecrows. Will the scarecrows come forward please.'

'Please,' said Susan to a very fat woman, 'may we
come past, *please?*' But the fat woman was deaf and her
neighbour seemed to be deaf too.

The clapping began again and it was much louder
than before.

'That means they're waiting for us and getting
impatient,' said John as he dodged under a clergy-
man's elbow.

People in front were laughing and clapping. People
behind were clapping and laughing too. At last John
and Susan managed to wriggle their way through to the
front, and were just going to cross the lawn when they
noticed two figures, one walking sideways and the other
one hopping towards the judge's table.

They were Worzel Gummidge and Earthy Mangold!

Earthy was still wearing her cobweb veil, though it
had got a little torn in places. Gummidge was as untidy
and muddy-looking as ever – especially as he was in his
shirt-sleeves.

'Thank ee' kindly,' said Earthy as a lady who was
standing behind a table put a large box of chocolates into
her twiggy little hands. 'Thank ee' kindly,' she said
again, and sat down with a jerk.

Two or three people hurried to pick her up.

'My poor child, I hope you haven't hurt yourself,' said
one of them. 'What a nasty tumble!'

"Tweren't a tumble!' said Earthy in her high cheerful

little voice. 'That were a curtsey. It's always a bit awkward trying to curtsey when your knees aren't jointed.'

Worzel Gummidge was pushing his way towards the table and now he snatched at the camera which was being held out to him and shambled away without a word of thanks. He was followed hoppingly by Earthy Mangold.

'He *is* rude,' whispered Susan.

'And I'll be blamed,' said John gloomily. 'I always am. It really is too bad of them to take our prizes.'

Gummidge and Earthy crossed the farther end of the lawn and pushed their way through the crowd. The children were much too shy to follow them, and because there were still more prizes to be given away they had to stand where they were, for more people were crowding up behind them.

Half an hour later they found the camera in the shrubbery. It was lying beside a heap of rather squashed looking chocolates. Evidently Earthy had taken a fancy to the box and the ribbon.

'Cheek!' said John, 'what frightful cheek to take our prizes.'

But they were so pleased with the camera and the chocolates that they really could not go on being cross with Gummidge and Earthy.

They walked back across the meadows to Scatterbrook because, as Susan said, it really was safer to leave Penfold before they got mixed up in any more scarecrow trouble. She had seen Mrs Bloomsbury-Barton among the crowd and was afraid that Gummidge might say something dreadful to her.

It had been rather a tiring day, so after they had scrubbed some of the stain from their hands and faces they were glad to sit on the low window seat of the parlour; there to read and munch chocolates and make plans about all the pictures they would take with the new camera.

Supper would be late, so Mrs Braithewaite told them, and they were full enough of chocolates to be glad about that. Pleasant sounds from the farm-yard and sweet scents from the garden joined together to make them feel happy. Susan stretched herself like a sleepy kitten. John curled up on the window-seat like a contented puppy. They were both nearly asleep when they heard the click-clacketing of high-heeled shoes coming up the flagged path. It was Mrs Bloomsbury-Barton, of course: nobody else's heels ever rapped out such an indignant tune on any path. The parlour door was open, so they couldn't help hearing what was being said.

'I know you do your best to look after the children, and I know that children will *be* children, but I must beg of you to send for John and Susan at once.'

'Send for them?' repeated Mrs Braithewaite. 'Why they've –' Mrs Bloomsbury-Barton went on talking.

'They behaved quite well at *first* except that perhaps they were not very polite at the prize-giving. But now they are behaving like a couple of hooligans.'

'*In*deed!' said Mrs Braithewaite, and John and Susan could hear from her voice that she was rather annoyed.

'Yes, "*indeed*",' said Mrs Bloomsbury-Barton. 'The Rector of Penfold has just rung me up. I agree with him that though there is no harm in children dressing-up as scarecrows there is no need for them to behave like savages. Ever since six o'clock John and Susan –'

'Won't you please step inside,' interrupted Mrs Braithewaite. There followed a tap-tapping noise and John and Susan looked solemnly down at their books as Mrs Bloomsbury-Barton's steps came nearer and nearer to the parlour door.

'And now,' said Mrs Braithewaite, 'and now perhaps

you will tell me what the children are supposed to have done?'

'The girl,' Mrs Bloomsbury-Barton's voice was quivering with rage, 'the girl has been walking about with a fowl on her head.'

'With a towel, did you say?' asked Mrs Braithewaite. 'I don't see any harm in that. No doubt the poor child was only trying to dress up like an Indian.'

'I did not say *towel*, I said *fowl*,' said Mrs Bloomsbury-Barton. John and Susan bit their lips as they looked at one another: it was so difficult to keep their laughter in.

'I said *fowl*,' repeated Mrs Bloomsbury-Barton, 'fowl – hen – chicken.'

'Well that's a funny thing to do,' snapped Mrs Braithewaite, 'that is a funny thing to do.'

'A very rude thing to do, an excessively impertinent thing to do. The girl Susan, who was dressed as a scarecrow, went up to a great many ladies and said that her hat was smarter than the ones they were wearing.'

'You don't say!' murmured Mrs Braithewaite.

'I simply say what I have heard.' The children could hear Mrs Bloomsbury-Barton tapping her umbrella on the stone-flagged passage. 'The rector has just rung me up to say that she was most insulting to any ladies who happened to be wearing feather-trimmed hats. She offered to sell them chickens or fowls or hens *instead*.'

Mrs Braithewaite made a clicking noise with her tongue.

Mrs Bloomsbury-Barton continued: 'The boy who was dressed as a scarecrow upset the bran-tub and stuffed his pockets with bran. He said he wanted the bran for a friend of his.'

'And when did all this happen?' asked Mrs Braithewaite.

'It is happening *now*.' Mrs Bloomsbury-Barton's

umbrella rapped three times on the stone floor. 'The rector has just rung me up to beg that you will send for the children at once. He can do nothing with them.'

There was a pause. John and Susan bit their lips harder than ever, and then Mrs Braithewaite spoke.

'Let me tell you,' she said. 'Let me tell you that the children came back at half-past five and they've been as quiet as mice ever since. I don't say they're always quiet, but fair is fair. Look for yourself.'

The steps came nearer, the parlour door was pushed further open and John and Susan stared down at their books. They heard a sort of gasp from Mrs Bloomsbury-Barton.

'That's where they've been since half-past five,' repeated Mrs Braithwaite, 'as good as gold both of them.'

'There must be some curious mistake.' Mrs Bloomsbury-Barton's voice sounded quite humble as she tip-toed away from the door. 'I must explain to the Rector.'

Neither John nor Susan ever knew what she did explain to the Rector, but what did it matter? Mrs Braithewaite gave them cream and blackcurrant jam on newly-baked bread for supper. For once, Worzel Gummidge had not got them into trouble for his own queer behaviour!

CHAPTER V

GUMMIDGE'S CLEVERNESS

—

It was nearly the end of hay harvest and everybody at Scatterbrook Farm was very busy. John and Susan had been up since early morning helping, hindering, and enjoying themselves. It had been fun to lead Biddy,

the old brown mare, up and down the narrow lane
while the cart creaked behind her and her hooves
powdered the dry mud of the ruts. It had been even
better fun when Bill, the farmhand, was leading her,
to lie on the very top of the swaying hay-load and
flatten themselves as the lowest branch of a sycamore
tree tried to comb their hair and the sky looked bluer
and nearer than usual. They did not know which
was nicer, the scents or the sounds. The smell of dried
clover and hot horse and oily leather was much pleasan-
ter to their noses than any of the things that rich people
buy to put on handkerchiefs. The whirring of a reaper
in a distant field, the swish-swish of hay tossing from the
pitchforks and the buzzing of flies made them feel
sleepy; so at about a quarter to twelve they left the
workers and sprawled against a haycock under cover
of the hedge.

Presently John closed his eyes while Susan rolled over
on to her front and peeped through her fingers at a
grasshopper that seemed too tired to hop and was
resting on a grass-blade.

'I didn't know they could keep still for so long,'
thought Susan. 'Perhaps it's sulking, like Gummidge.'
Then she shut her eyes too, and began to dream about
the scarecrow. She dreamed they were back in London
again and that Gummidge was driving a bus very
very fast round Piccadilly Circus. As he drove he sang,
'Here we go round the mulberry bush,' and then he
turned into a sheep and kept taking his hat on and off.
Every time he raised it, he coughed. It seemed perfectly
natural as dreams always do. So when some sudden
sound jerked her awake she was not surprised, when
she had got used to the sunlight again, to see Gummidge sitting with his back to the hedge. A red cotton
handkerchief was spread over his knobbly knees and

he was pouring something from a lemonade bottle
on to the grass. When he had emptied it, he glanced
at Susan and smiled, but very slowly, of course, because
the skin of his face was so stiff. As usual when he smiled,
little trickles of dried mud ran out from the wrinkles
of his turnip face.

'Sulking, eh?' he asked. 'Having a good long sulk, are
you?'

'Of course I'm not sulking,' said Susan indignantly.
'I've been asleep and dreaming about you.'

'Ooh aye! I dream sometimes,' said Gummidge.
'Sometimes I dreams it's raining and then when I wakes
I finds it is. 'Taint everyone can do that.'

'I should think anyone could do it if they slept out-of-
doors,' said Susan. 'I mean the rain would wake them.'

'Trouble is they don't all sleep out o' doors,' replied
Gummidge reasonably.

The sound of their voices disturbed John who now
sat upright, blinking first at the sunlight and then at
Worzel Gummidge.

The scarecrow smiled at him but a little less stiffly now
because his face had had some practice.

'Once I dreamed I were the King,' he announced.

'Our King?' asked Susan, 'Do you mean the King of
England?' She giggled a little because she had once
seen the procession before the Opening of Parliament
and it was difficult to think of Gummidge sitting in a
royal coach.

'I means the Scarecrow King,' said Gummidge.

'Is there one?' John asked.

'Used to be two,' Gummidge told him. 'Trouble was
they both got sick and tired of not having brims so they
both gave up in a temper.'

'Brims?' repeated Susan in her most puzzled voice.

'I said brims and I means brims.' Gummidge removed

his hat and tapped the top of it. 'This here's the crown and t'other part's the brim. When t'other part of this falls off then I'll be King.' He put the hat back on his head, sighed and remarked, 'It's cruel work being a King – no shade and no shelter. Not but what a crown's useful for keepin' things in if it's not a tight fit. It's good for mushrooming too if you haven't got a handker-cher.'

As he finished speaking Gummidge picked up the red handkerchief from his knees and stuffed it into his pocket. The empty bottle went into the other pocket, but Susan and John were too interested in hearing about royal scarecrows to notice what he was doing.

'It seems all upside down somehow,' said Susan, 'I mean I think the brim ought to be the crown.'

'What you think's daft,' replied Gummidge, but in quite an amiable voice.

'It isn't daft!' put in John. 'It isn't daft at all. In all the pictures I've ever seen the crowns of kings and queens look much more like brims than hat-crowns.'

'That's all you know about it,' snapped Gum-midge. 'There aren't no pictures of scarecrow kings and queens.'

As neither John nor Susan could say they had ever seen a picture of a scarecrow king or queen they didn't say anything. Gummidge went on talking.

'When I'm king I'll make a lot of new laws. I'll make a law that all rooks is to have black wings. And –'

'They have black wings already,' interrupted John.

Gummidge took no notice.

'And I'll make a law that all rabbits is to live in burrows and all bats is to fly and that rain's to be wet and sun's to be hot and –'

'But whatever's the use of making laws about things that can't help happening?' asked Susan.

'So as nobody can break the laws o' course,' said
Gummidge. 'I'll make lots of laws that can't be broken
and then nobody can't defy me.'

'It doesn't seem sense,' said Susan.

'It seems a lot o' sense,' contradicted Gummidge.
'If I makes laws that can't be broke then I'll be a good
king.'

John and Susan felt that there might be something
wrong with this argument, and wrinkled up their fore-
heads as they tried to think of an answer. Susan stared
at a beetle while she thought and John gazed at a grasshopper; so for a minute or two neither of them noticed
what Gummidge was doing until his creaking and
rustling disturbed them.

'Gummidge!' said Susan suddenly – 'You mustn't
do that.' For Worzel Gummidge had wriggled a few
yards away from them and was now tugging savagely
at the knots of a red handkerchief in which Bill's dinner
was packed. Bill was one of the farm men.

'I must do what I wants,' said Gummidge, pulling
out some bread and cheese sandwiches. Before Susan
or John could stop him he had pushed them down a
rabbit hole.

'Mustn't take those home,' he muttered. 'If Hannah
got at 'em she'd have the mice worser nor ever.
And there's no sense in not carrying extra weight
neither.'

As he spoke, he unscrewed the top from another
bottle, and poured cold tea out on to the ground.

'Gummidge!' gasped John, 'That's Bill's tea.'

'And you spoiled his dinner!' gasped Susan.

'He's welcome to both. I only wants the bottles and
the handkerchers.'

Gummidge stuffed the other handkerchief into his
pocket and smiled happily at the bottle.

'But he can't eat sandwiches from a rabbit-hole and, anyway, you've squashed them all up.'

Susan's voice was very indignant, but Gummidge's was quite calm as he answered. 'If he can't he can't. I'll be getting along now. Earthy she *will* be set up when she sees these glassy ornments and the handkerchers. Good mornin'.'

Gummidge creaked up to his feet and walked sideways towards a gap in the hedge. The children let him go. It seemed the only thing to do; besides they could hear a murmur of voices which probably meant that the men had knocked off work and would be coming in search of their dinners. They listened again: yes, the whirring of the reaper had stopped: that meant it must be twelve o'clock.

'We'd better go away, I think, or we'll only be asked awkward questions,' said John.

They had just reached the gap in the hedge and decided to go through it when they heard a shout.

'Bother!' said Susan. 'Now I suppose somebody *will* ask questions.'

But it was only Farmer Braithewaite, calling to them from the gate and asking them to go back to the farm and remind Mrs Braithewaite to collect all the eggs as soon as possible.

'Just as well!' remarked John, as they walked rather dawdlingly along the lane. 'Now perhaps we'll be able to keep out of the way until after the men's dinner hour. They won't be able to ask questions, and they'll have forgotten about it by the time we get back.'

'I don't think people do forget about dinners they haven't had,' argued Susan.

Their plan about staying at the farm for an hour was a failure. They thought it had begun well when Susan offered to help to collect the eggs and Mrs

Braithewaite said she would be glad if they would because she was going to be busy in the dairy. But just as they were crossing the yard with their baskets, she came bustling after them.

'I'll be forgetting my own head next,' she said. 'Mr Crump from Penfold brought a note for Mr Braithewaite half an hour back and he wants an answer as soon as possible. You take it to the harvest field as soon as you can, there's good children. I'll get the eggs collected.'

Mrs Braithewaite smiled so kindly at them that it was impossible to refuse, especially when she added, 'I've got a treat for you to-day. I'm sending your dinners out to the field for you, so you needn't come back to the house.'

They thanked her and hoped they sounded pleased, but they felt too worried to be really excited about treats. Worzel Gummidge would certainly be getting into trouble again and when he was in trouble they always seemed to share it.

When they returned to the field they heard at once that something had gone wrong. Farmer Braithewaite was standing with his back to a gate and he was arguing with two of the men – Bill and Dick.

'All I can say is if you've not got the sense to remember where you put your dinners, it's no use blaming me.'

'Just over by that haycock they were,' said Bill, pointing towards the place where John and Susan had been sitting and where Worzel Gummidge had done his bad deed for the day. 'Just by that bramble bush our dinners were. I knows that hedge same as I knows the palm of my own hand.'

The farmer gave the sort of grunt which meant he didn't care. 'Dinners don't walk,' he said.

'They've been stolen,' argued Dick.

Just then the farmer turned round and noticed John and Susan. He began to read the note from Mr Crump of Penfold and before he had finished it Bill gave a roar. 'There he goes, see. There he goes!'

'I don't see nobody,' said Dick, looking from east to west.

'Not there, *there!*' shouted Bill. 'He's creeping along the hedge.'

'I don't see nobody,' repeated Dick, looking this time slowly from west to east, then down at his boots, and then up at the sky.

'Course you don't see nobody – not now,' said Bill savagely. 'He's gone now. Went through that gap in the hedge. He'd all but reached it when I saw him.'

'Saw who?' asked Farmer Braithewaite, glancing up from his note.

'I don't know who, sir,' answered Bill. 'A nasty-looking tramp-man he was with a black hat. And he's got a bottle in his hand and red handkerchiefs sticking out of his coat pockets.'

'I didn't see nobody,' said Dick obstinately.

'I did and I'm after him.' Bill snatched up a pitch-fork and began to lumber up the sloping field towards the gap in the hedge. Dick followed, grumbling a good deal. After Bill came Farmer Braithewaite with John and Susan a pace or two behind.

They too had seen what Bill had seen – Worzel Gummidge (who had probably returned to the field to look for more handkerchiefs) sidling along in his crab-like way in the shadow of the hedge. His back had been turned and he was, as Bill said, carrying a bottle. They too had seen the red handkerchiefs flapping from his coat pockets before he had disappeared through the gap in the hedge.

'Go it, Bill!' jeered Dick.

Bill pounded on up the slope of the hill, and suddenly John decided to try to overtake him. On and on ran the party, dodging haycocks and occasionally bumping into one another.

John reached the gap first and Susan only two seconds later. They were just in time to see Worzel Gummidge take his four or five last steps across a small field and turn through a gateway before the sound of heavy breathing and a shout of 'Oi!' told them that Bill had seen Gummidge too.

'What did I say?' he asked.

'I didn't see nobody,' persisted Dick, who had now joined them.

'That's because you were too slow,' jeered Bill. 'I can see him now. Least, I can see the top of his hat. He's turned left down the lane, leading to the allotment gardens.'

Bill was quite right. The hedge was cut low in places and every now and then Worzel Gummidge's hat could be seen quite distinctly. He seemed to be walking faster than usual.

'I'm after him,' said Bill for the second time, and the race began again. The second field sloped down hill and it was only a small one too. Yet when they had all turned into the lane there was no sign of Worzel Gummidge.

'I don't see nobody,' panted Dick.

'He'll be round the next bend,' said Bill, as he started down the lane.

'I don't see no sense in goin' on,' said Dick; and, even though they had never liked him very much, the children felt that they loved him then. John decided to give him his favourite tie and Susan wondered if he liked toffee.

'Oi!' shouted Dick. 'Come back.'

But Bill did not even turn his head, so a grumbling farm-hand, two anxious children and a very hot farmer followed him.

After they had hurried round the bend in the lane the children held their breath for a second or two (not for longer because they had been running too hard).

'Seems Bill were right after all,' remarked Dick slowly. Bill had been perfectly right. There, sitting by the side of the road, his back against a sandy bank and his legs stuck straight out in front of him in the grass, sat Worzel Gummidge, the scarecrow. A red handkerchief was still sticking out of his pocket, an empty bottle was lying by his side and his hat was tipped over one eye.

'Oi!' shouted Bill.

'Hi!' shouted Dick.

'Now then, what's all this?' asked the farmer.

Worzel Gummidge did not answer – nor did he move – not even when a dead leaf drifted down from the hedge and settled on his nose.

'Oh! I daren't look,' whispered Susan, as Bill pushed his pitchfork towards Worzel Gummidge. 'Oh! I can't bear to look.'

She covered her face with both hands and even John turned his head away.

Bill's voice sounded louder and louder, angrier and angrier, and then suddenly Dick gave a roar of laughter.

'Tramp indeed!' he said. 'That's nobbut the old scarecrow that we used to set up in Ten-acre Field.'

'So it is,' agreed the farmer.

'Scarecrows don't walk,' Bill argued. 'I tells you I saw him walking along in front of me, and then all of a sudden he sat down. Scarecrows don't sit down. I'll show you if he's a scarecrow or not.'

The prongs of the pitchfork were very near to Worzel Gummidge now. Before they turned away, John and Susan gave one more glance at him. He was still smiling and his face looked more turnipy than ever.

'I'll show you,' repeated Bill.

'Steady on now,' said the farmer and Susan rushed at him crying. 'Don't let him hurt him! Oh! please don't let him hurt him.'

The farmer stepped forward; and then there came a yell – the sort of roaring furious yell that might be expected from any scarecrow that has been prodded in the middle. There was another yell and then another one.

'I'll be bothered!' said the farmer.

John who was the first of the children to look towards Gummidge whispered to Susan. 'It's all right. I tell you, it's perfectly all right. *Gummidge* is all right.'

Gummidge, so far as they could see, *was* perfectly all right. But it was not easy to see properly. They could just see bits of his black form through a whirling black and golden cloud. The cloud buzzed angrily.

'Stirred up a wasp's nest – that's what Bill's done,' remarked Dick slowly. 'Just look at him now.'

Bill was breaking his way through the hedge and back into the field they had just crossed. Tiny clouds had broken away from the big cloud of wasps. Bill had taken off his cap and was beating the insects back.

'Best be going back to the field, I should say,' remarked Dick as a wasp buzzed crossly against his own nose. 'Tramp indeed. I'd like to see the tramp that would go on sitting among *that* lot. Best be getting back now.'

The others thought so too.

Half way up the slope, Susan stopped. 'Don't let's go back to the farm,' she said. 'Let's go to the orchard and eat plums and those little crispy early apples.'

So they went to the orchard and ate so many apples and plums that they forgot all about dinner, though the sight of a wasp, buzzing round a windfall apple, re-minded Susan again of Worzel Gummidge.

'I suppose,' she said, 'I suppose the wasps haven't built a nest *in* Gummidge.'

"Course not!' said John. 'Wasps' nests take a long time to build.'

'So do robins' nests, and he had one in his pocket last year.'

'That's different,' said John.

'Well if one sort of thing likes building nests in you another sort of thing might like it too.' Susan picked up another plum. 'And wasps eat fruit and I don't want them to eat Gummidge.'

'Gummidge isn't fruit.'

'But he's vegetable, at least sort of vegetable. Wasps may *like* turnips.'

'I don't mind if they do,' said John lazily.

And then because it was so very hot and they were so very full of apples and plums they fell asleep again.

CHAPTER VI

TWO RED HANDKERCHIEFS

—

JOHN and Susan did not go back to the harvest field after tea because they discovered that the tortoiseshell cat was keeping a family of four kittens in the hay-loft, and they had all reached the running-about stage. There was a black one with white feet, a white one with a black tip to its tail, a red and golden one that was as gay to look at as the marigolds under the kitchen window, and a small tortoiseshell, whose coat reminded them of the patchwork quilt in Emily's room. The tortoiseshell was the most exciting of all. When it was touched it fluffed up its fur and scratched and then, making noises like fizzy lemonade when the stopper of the bottle is unscrewed, raced up to the rafters.

They stayed with the kittens until they heard the creaking of the hay-wagons and the clanking of buckets in the yard below and knew that the last load of the hay had been carried and that the horses were being watered. Then they played a game they had invented for themselves when they first came to stay in the country, closing their eyes (though this wasn't necessary up in the loft) and guessing by sound what was happening down below.

'That's Dick crossing the yard,' said Susan.

'No,' argued John, 'that's Bill. Listen, he'll stamp his boots on the flagstones by the pump: he always does.'

The ring of nailed boots on the flags showed he was right.

'He was carrying two buckets,' said Susan. 'He put one down just two seconds before the other.'

'Not so sure,' said John. 'I'm not *certain*; so it will be half a point to you if you win.'

There followed the squeak of the pump handle, the sound of pouring water, the clank of a bucket handle and – yes – again the squeak of the pump.

They were rather good at the game by now and could tell what was happening almost as well as by looking through the dusty loft windows.

They knew that Lizzy, whom they always called the goosegirl because of her pigtails and bare legs, had come scurrying into the stable below to talk to Bill and Dick.

'You ought to have seen him running away from those

wasps,' said Dick. 'Laugh? I could have cracked my sides laughing.'

He told the story of Bill and Gummidge while Susan and John kept their mouths very close to the kittens' soft fur so that their giggles should be muffled.

'Scarecrow or not!' said Bill obstinately. 'I'd swear I saw the fellow moving, and I saw him plop down by the side of the hedge.'

Dick and Lizzy laughed so loudly that John and Susan were able to join in.

'And the best part of it was,' said Dick, 'the best part of it was that when we came back to the field the first thing I saw were the dinners – just where we'd left 'em – tied up in the red handkerchiefs with the tea bottles beside them.'

'They weren't there when I first went to look for them, that I do know,' said Bill sulkily.

'Something wrong with your eyesight, that's all,' said Dick. 'First of all you can't see things that are there and then you see tramps that turn into scarecrows.'

During the laughter that followed, Susan whispered to John. 'Do you know I believe Gummidge must have *repented* and gone back to the place where we were sitting to *return* the dinner.'

'Don't be silly,' said John. 'You can't put tea that's been spilled back into the bottles again. And you can't mend squashed sandwiches.'

'You never quite know what scarecrows can do, especially Gummidge.'

'*Think*, silly!' said John. 'We *saw* the handkerchiefs sticking out of Gummidge's pocket before the wasps got angry.'

While Susan was thinking and puzzling and getting more and more bewildered, the people went on laughing.

'Well, all's well that ends well,' said Lizzy. 'I hope the dinners were good when you did get them.'

'I should say they were,' said Bill.

'Prime!' agreed Dick. 'Mrs Braithewaite *can* cut sandwiches.'

There was a general sound of bustling down below, as Bill and Dick hung up the horse-collars and Lizzy said she must be off.

'Well!' said Susan at last, 'that's one of the greatest mysteries of Scatterbrook.'

'Easy!' said John, 'I've got it. There was a reaper going in a field that doesn't belong to Farmer Braithewaite. Gummidge must have taken the dinners belonging to some other men and put them back in our field and then Dick and Bill found them again.'

'P'raps he was pretending to be Robin Hood,' said Susan, who always tried to find excuses for Worzel Gummidge. '*You* know – robbing the rich to give to the poor – sort of thing.'

'I'd like to see Gummidge dressed in Lincoln green,' laughed John. They went on talking about Gummidge for a long time until John pulled his big gun-metal watch from a pocket, looked at it, scowled, shook it, and put it to his ear.

'My inside-clock says supper-time.'

'So does mine,' agreed Susan.

'But it isn't.' John put the watch back into his pocket. 'I'd hoped my inside-clock might be right and my watch might have stopped, but it hasn't. I'm frightfully hungry. Let's see if we can have supper now.'

Mrs Braithewaite was quite pleased to give them early supper. As she said, though not very politely, it 'got them out of the way in nice time.'

But Susan and John were not offended because the new bread smelled so good and the fresh butter looked

so golden and there was an inch of cream on the top of
the milk.

'Anyone would think you'd not had a meal for a
week,' she remarked cheerfully, as John passed up his
plate for a third pasty. 'Still, I always say that harvesting
is hungry work. And that reminds me, did you remember
to bring back those two red handkerchiefs and the empty
bottles?'

John's mouth was too full of pasty for him to be able
to answer properly. Susan's was too full of lemon curd
tart, but they both turned crimson in the face as they
stared first at Mrs Braithewaite and then at each other.
It was such a very odd question. Did she know about
Gummidge?

'Um-m, no,' said John at last.

'You see, we *couldn't*,' explained Susan who had not
taken such a big mouthful as her brother. 'Because you
see –'

Luckily Mrs Braithewaite interrupted –

'I thought as much. I never did see such careless
children in all my born days. There was I taking all
the trouble to cut sandwiches and do them up in red
cotton handkerchiefs as a surprise for you, and so
that you could think you were being real harvesters,
and you can't even remember to act like real
harvesters and bring the handkerchiefs and the bottles
back.'

This was dreadful –

'I – I – we're sorry!' gulped Susan, who was just
beginning to understand what might have happened.

'Sorry won't bring back my handkerchiefs or the
bottles. You'll have to go back to the field and fetch
them after supper. I suppose you *found* them quite
easily? Lizzy said there was nobody in the field when
she went there so she put your dinners under that

big beech tree where you always sit. She said you'd be bound to find them. Did you?'

The children didn't answer but, luckily for them, the kettle on the hob did. Its lid began to bob frantically up and down and a spurt of water shot from the spout and on to Mrs Braithewaite's newly polished fender. Up she jumped to fetch a duster.

Susan looked gratefully at the kettle and noticed for the first time that it had a nice kindly shape. She had never liked it much before because of its unfriendly way of suddenly spouting boiling water on to bare knees or letting scalding steam find a passing arm. It had been a horrid kettle before, but Susan loved it now, as Mrs Braithewaite dumped it on to the side of the stove. But even the kindly kettle could not save the children from the next question –

'Were the sandwiches good?' asked Mrs Braithewaite.

She had turned to John who was always the hungrier of the two.

He paused to lick a crumb from his upper lip, looked nervously at Susan, and answered: 'Prime!'

'Yours too?' asked Mrs Braithewaite. 'I remembered you don't like mustard.'

Susan remembered too what Dick and Bill had said about the sandwiches which were to have been her dinner and John's. After all it was possible to be truthful without giving Gummidge away.

'Mrs Braithewaite *can* cut sandwiches,' she answered in the sort of voice that people use when they are repeating poetry.

Mrs Braithewaite smiled, Susan went very red, and John asked, 'Can we go now, please?'

'Yes,' was the answer, 'You'd better go and get those handkerchiefs.'

It was all very well to be asked to go and get hand-kerchiefs from the pocket of a scarecrow who might be still sitting in a cloud of wasps or who might be anywhere within two miles, but Susan and John were glad to leave the kitchen so that they could talk things over.

Of course, they both understood by now that Bill and Dick had eaten *their* dinners and returned *their* handker-chiefs and that Gummidge was not very likely to give up the handkerchiefs or bottles that he had taken.

'Still, we must go and ask him,' said John. 'Only supposing he's sulky and won't answer.'

'And supposing we have to go all through those thousands and millions of wasps,' said Susan.

'Well, I just won't,' said John.

'Then we'll have to explain, and it is so awfully difficult to have to explain about Gummidge.' Susan walked rather miserably through the farm-yard gate; and she didn't say any more after that until they paused at the entrance to the harvest field where John, after wrapping a nearly white handkerchief round his wrist, stopped to grub up a bunch of tall nettles.

'What for?' asked Susan.

'Well, nettles sting and wasps sting, and if we have to have a battle we had better be armed.'

After all though, there was no need to be armed. By the time they reached the place where they had last seen Worzel Gummidge there were only a very few wasps in sight and these were buzzing distractedly round a burned and blackened hole in the bank. Somebody had taken the wasps' nest and Worzel Gummidge had gone.

'Perhaps they've taken him too,' said Susan miserably. 'I mean, supposing the nest was in Gummidge's tummy they may have burnt him too.'

'I don't believe Gummidge would let himself be burned,' answered John consolingly.

'You never know. Sometimes he says he feels so reckless he doesn't care what he does.'

Susan gave a little shiver because the sun had gone down below the highest hayfields quite a long time ago, and she was in her thinnest cotton frock.

They called to Gummidge, but there was no answer, and then they hunted through two or three fields; but never a cough nor glimpse of a bowler hat told them that he was near.

'It's all no use,' said John at last. 'We'd better go home, but I don't know what we're going to say to Mrs Braithewaite.'

As a matter of fact, there was no need to say anything at all to Mrs Braithewaite, because by the time they came back to the farm the kitchen was quite full of excited-looking people who were all talking at once.

The most excited of all was a red-haired girl in khaki shorts who kept on saying that she wasn't used to the country and that she was so upset she didn't know what to do. The next excited was a fair-haired young man in spectacles. He wore khaki shorts too and his teeth stuck out in quite a frightening way every time he announced that he knew the law of the land as well as anybody and he knew that anybody who put a dangerous bull in a field without putting up a notice-board to say that the animal was dangerous ought to be prosecuted.

Then Farmer Braithewaite, who was almost as excited as the strangers, said that trespassers ought to be prosecuted *always* and that anyway there was a notice in his field saying 'Beware of the Bull,' and added 'Can't you read?'

The young man said he could read and that he could write letters to lawyers too.

John and Susan slipped into the kitchen and sat down in the window seat, very quietly for fear they should be sent away because it was all being so exciting and it was fun to hear grown-up people quarrelling. All the same, it was difficult, without asking questions, to find out what all the trouble was about, and rather like missing the beginning of a play.

'Anyway,' said Farmer Braithewaite, knocking out his pipe on the hearthstone as though it were the tobacco's fault. 'Anyway, let me tell you that my bull is *not* savage or dangerous – a more peaceful creature never breathed.'

'Of course he's savage!' shouted the girl with the red hair. 'You just ought to have seen the look he gave me. It made my blood run cold. And then he followed, breathing hot breath down my neck, ramping and rampaging like a mad thing.'

Susan giggled because it was so difficult to think of anything as lumbering and gentle as the old red bull ramping *or* rampaging, and Lizzy, the goosegirl, murmured, 'It must have been the red hair he didn't like.'

'You go and scald the churns in the dairy,' said Mrs Braithewaite.

As soon as Lizzy had gone, the farmer told Dick, the farm-hand, to go to the long meadow and make sure that the notice-board was still in place.

It seemed a long time before they heard the clump-clump of his returning boots on the flagstones of the garden path, but during that time Mrs Braithewaite had boiled a kettle and made tea for the two strangers (because she was very kind really).

'Well?' asked Farmer Braithewaite as Dick came into the room.

'Well, it's a queer thing that is,' the farmhand's voice

was slower than ever. 'It's a very queer thing. That notice-board was there this afternoon. Bill and me both saw it, didn't we, Bill?'

'Yes,' agreed Bill. 'We both saw it.'

'And it was there yesterday,' went on Dick, 'but it's not there now.'

'I don't believe it ever was there,' said the girl with the red hair. 'And the way that creature came at me sniffing and braying –'

'Bulls don't bray,' a slow smile spread over Dick's face. 'Braying's left to other sort of creatures. And anyone could tell, anyone who knew anything about country ways, that the board and the post's only been wrenched up lately. It's like this – there was an ant's nest where the post was stuck in.'

'My good fellow,' remarked the young man with the spectacles. 'My good fellow, we are talking about bulls and not about ants.'

Dick did not answer. He was, John noticed, just a little like Worzel Gummidge to look at and a little like him to listen to.

'The ants are still bustling about and carrying their grubs to another place,' he said. 'It's getting late and they would all be asleep ordinarily, so that shows that the post with the notice-board must have been pulled up this evening.'

'I think,' said Susan, quite forgetting that sometimes it was really better scarcely to be seen and not heard at all, 'I think that when ants are carrying their grubs about they look awfully like washerwomen with big bundles of clothes.'

Mrs Braithewaite saw her, saw John, and told both of them it was long past their bedtime.

So they did not know what happened after that in the farm kitchen.

CHAPTER VII

THE CARETAKER

—

THE next morning, John and Susan were awakened by unusual noises in the farm-yard below their bedroom windows. They were used to the clanging of milk-pails, the squeak of the pump, rumblings of carts, tramping of feet, and all the clucking and gobbling, quacking and mooing, crowing and whinnying that made a waking-up tune in the mornings. But they were not used to strange voices shouting to know if anybody was in.

Susan tiptoed out of bed and put her head through the open window. A furniture van with a London name, painted in gold letters, was outside the gate. The driver, who had switched off his engine, was talking loudly to Farmer Braithewaite.

'Very sorry to trouble you, I'm sure,' he said. 'But as we're strangers here and as we were told you are a farmer we thought we'd better come to you about it. We don't want to run the risk of being gored by mad bulls and it does seem a peculiar thing for an old lady to want to keep a bull in her garden.'

The farmer opened his mouth but, before he could say a word, the lorry-driver, who seemed to be very good at making long speeches, went on:

'It's like this, we arrived here early bringing a load of furniture for the White House and with the key which we had from the owner with special instructions to lock up afterwards because she won't be coming down till this evening. And what do you think we saw?'

Once more Farmer Braithewaite opened his mouth

and this time he shook his head too, but he was not given a chance to speak.

'Leaning up against the front gate was a notice saying "Beware of the Bull." Well, that's a nice thing to expect to find in any lady's front garden. I've suffered a lot in the course of my duties, been bit by parrots and even by a monkey once. That's all in the game if you happen to be a removal man. And I've had to lend my cap to carry kittens in and I've given seed to canaries and been licked at by Pekingese, but I do bar bulls – and that's a fact.' The indignant little man drew a long breath and then asked several questions without waiting for the answers.

'What would you do about it? Would you stand being gored by bulls and most likely sent crashing through mirrors that you chanced to be carrying into the house? Wouldn't you think you'd a right to ask the reason why ladies wants to keep bulls in their gardens? It must be a bad sort of bull too. There isn't only the notice-board against the gate: there's a red flag on each gate-post too – just by way of extra warning I suppose. Well, I calls 'em flags but really they look more like red handkerchiefs fixed on to sticks, and the sticks are standing in bottles.'

Susan didn't wait to hear any more, but she hurried into the passage where she collided with John, who had also been leaning out of his bedroom window.

'It's Gummidge, of course,' she gasped. 'He's fond of notice-boards. He must have put the bull one on the gate of the White House, and he must have used the handkerchiefs as flags.'

'And we'll be blamed,' said John. 'We always are. Oh! bother Worzel Gummidge! Let's get dressed quickly.'

Five minutes later, having tip-toed out through the front door, they were running up the village street.

The White House had been empty for months, but now it had been bought by somebody whose name was Miss Duffy. The children had heard quite a lot about her from Mrs Perkins, the Vicar's wife, and she sounded nice.

There was a high wall all round the garden of the White House and there was a double wooden gate of the solid sort that can't be looked through.

The sight of the notice-board which had been propped up from inside, so that the warning showed above this prim gate, made Susan want to giggle: so did the empty bottles, and the red handkerchief flags fluttering above the gate-posts.

Luckily the gate was not locked. John turned the ring handle, pushed and went into the garden, followed by Susan.

Evidently Gummidge had been there because a little trail of strange objects lay on the gravelled drive. There was some putty, a cigarette end, an empty sardine tin, some pieces of orange peel, a hen's feather, and a few lumps of mud.

'Gummidge has been turning out his pockets, I should think,' remarked Susan.

'He must have done it last night then. This feather's simply sopping with dew.' John flicked a damp and draggled feather against his sister's cheek.

The front door was locked and so was the back one. Every window on the ground floor was fastened and shuttered.

'If Gummidge has got in, I should think we can,' sighed Susan.

'But we don't know for certain that he has got in,' objected John. 'He may have gone away again.'

A sheep-like cough contradicted him, and the cough seemed to come from under his feet.

The children looked down, and noticed that they were standing on an iron grating. When they knelt down they saw that this had been loosened lately and that beneath it was a dark square hole.

'There's a thing like this at the farm,' said John; 'It's just above the cellar window. Farmer Braithewaite told me that it's used instead of a door when people want to put beer barrels in the cellar.'

He tugged at the grating and Susan helped. Presently they had dragged it clear of the hole and John hopped down among the dust and dried leaves at the bottom of the square hole.

'There's a shutter here,' he said, as he pulled at a little catch. 'I bet you anything that it opens into a cellar.'

It did open into a cellar. Three moments later John and Susan had left the sunlight above them and were standing with their feet on cool bricks.

'Quickly!' said Susan. 'We'd better shut ourselves in. Somebody is opening the front gate.'

John closed the wooden shutter with what he hoped was not a bang and then the children listened to the sounds of a lorry and voices shouting to one another, to the tramping of feet on gravel and many bumpings and bangings about.

'I suppose we're in the cellar,' whispered Susan. 'I do wish it wasn't so pitch dark.' She began to feel her way round the wall, but before she had taken more than two or three steps she trod on something that was soft and, at the same time, knobbly in places.

'Sorry!' said the something, and she recognized the wistful little voice of Hannah Harrow.

'Ooh aye! Course you're in the cellar,' said another voice (Worzel Gummidge's). 'Not that you've a right to be. Folks that have manners always knocks. And folks that have more manners don't come disturbin' other folks in the middle of the night.'

'It isn't the middle of the night,' said John.

'Don't talk daft. Nights is dark, days is light and it's dark now. I'm going to sleep till dawn. So there.'

If they could have found Worzel Gummidge they would have shaken him, but the cellar was pitch-dark and the floor was uneven besides being rather slippery. They begged him in whispers to answer but they dare not talk loudly because the tramping of feet above them told that the men had unlocked the front door and were carrying furniture in from the lorry. It was all very awkward and it was just a little frightening too. The noises outside and above them were so loud, Gummidge's breathing sounded very fast asleep and it was terribly dark.

Suddenly a particularly loud and clattering bang made Susan give a little scream.

'Oh! what was that?'

'I bumped my head,' muttered John. 'I bumped it on a beastly bit of jutting out wall.'

'Silly! your head isn't made of iron.' Susan was almost crying by now. 'I don't care if we are caught. I'm going to open the shutter just a chink and let some light in. I *must!*'

But Susan could not find the shutter; neither could John. The cellars of the White House were very big ones. The children groped their way round the walls. Sometimes they met in doorways that had no doors, sometimes they grazed their elbows on the stone shelves of winebins and sometimes they brushed their eyelashes against soft thick cobwebs.

And then suddenly John's fingers felt something familiar, he pressed, and in a second the cellar in which they were standing was lit up.

'Electric light! Oh! good,' breathed Susan.

When their eyes had grown used to the sudden change from darkness, the children saw a strange sight –

Earthy Mangold was surrounded by the framework of an old deck-chair. Evidently the canvas had given way and she had not bothered to get up. She was wearing her brown sacking cloak and her little blue and white apron.

'Mornin',' she said pleasantly. 'I've never known the sun get up so quickly. Shrunk too, hasn't it?' She lifted a twiggy hand and pointed to the electric light bulb.

John and Susan did not answer because they were staring at Worzel Gummidge who was lying on a bed that was made entirely of bottle-straws.

'Boots!' he said, patting some of the bottle-straws. 'Dozens and hundreds and thousands o' pairs o' boots. They all fits a treat. I'll have a new pair every day if I likes. Where's my hairbrush?'

'Plaguing the life out of me, Mr Gummidge,' said a sad resentful voice. 'It thinks it knows the way my hair ought to go but the hair thinks different.'

The voice, which was Hannah Harrow's, came from a rather dim corner of the cellar where the scarecrow lay face downwards on a piece of matting. Some of the strands of her tarred-string hair trailed in untidy wisps across the floor; and Gummidge's hedgehog was twisting about in the rest of it. Every now and then Hannah gave a little gasp of pain.

Susan felt really sorry for her. There were times when her own hair wanted to go in a different direction from the brush and comb's.

'Give it here then,' said Gummidge. 'Go and find a hairbrush of your own if you wants it.'

'I don't,' whispered Hannah. 'Really, I don't, Mr

Gummidge. The hairbrush found my hair. It's been at it all night, very near.'

'Wearing itself out, just when I wants it,' grumbled Gummidge. Certainly Worzel Gummidge did look rather as if he needed a hairbrush. So many spiders' webs covered his green sprouting hair that he seemed to be wearing a thick grey wig, and looked very very much older.

'Give it here,' repeated Gummidge impatiently.

'Oh! never mind your hair now,' said John rather crossly. 'Tell us what you're doing here.'

'I've taken on the job of caretaker here,' said Gummidge. 'It's a grand life. No worries and no rooks.'

'But who gave you the job?' asked Susan.

'I *took* it. That's what I said, didn't I? Nobody gave it to me.'

Gummidge snatched up another bottle-straw and began to put it on to his broom-stick leg.

'But this house belongs to Miss Duffy, and there'll be a frightful row when you're found out,' said Susan.

'That's all you knows. Folks isn't so daft nor so ungrateful neither as to make rows if other folks takes care of their houses. And after all the trouble I've took too, puttin' up notice-boards.'

Gummidge began to look sulky, as he put on another boot.

'But why did you put up that notice-board?'

'To keep folks out, of course. I've always been a noticing sort of fellow and I've noticed when you writes up "Beware of the Bull", it do keep folks out.'

'But you've been keeping out the men who have brought Miss Duffy's furniture,' argued John.

'*They* can come if they likes. I could do with a bit more furniture maybe – not but what we're comfortable enough.'

The cellar did not look very comfortable. There were a few packing cases, a rusty iron fender, a barrel or two, some empty bottles, Earthy's deck chair, Gummidge's stray bed and a few other odds and ends.

Susan and John both thought that it would be better not to tell Worzel Gummidge that his notice-board had failed to keep the furniture removal men out of Miss Duffy's house. The bumpings and bangings had stopped now, and they guessed that the men might have gone away to have breakfast.

It would be dreadful if Gummidge moved drawing-room furniture into the cellar or kitchen things into the bathroom.

'Don't you think you'd better come away now?' asked Susan coaxingly.

For answer, Gummidge got stiffly to his feet, sidled towards where Hannah was lying and picked up the hairbrush. Quite a lot of Hannah's hair came with it, but though she gave several protesting little shrieks, Gummidge took no notice and continued to tug.

A few strands came away altogether, and these Gummidge untwisted from among the hedgehog's bristles before using them as laces to fasten his new bottle-straw boots.

Then he brushed his hair with the hedgehog. The little creature did not seem to mind, but the children felt sorry for it as they saw it change from brown to cob-web grey while Gummidge's sprouting locks turned from grey to their usual cheerful green. When he put the hedgehog down it crawled away quite quickly and hid under a piece of sacking.

'I think,' said Susan, 'I think we'd better be getting back to breakfast before they miss us at the farm.'

'And you'd better come out of the cellar before any-body catches you,' said John to Gummidge.

'Folks only catch folks that are running away,' answered Gummidge. 'They don't catch folks at a sit-still.'

He flopped down again on to his straw bed.

'Boots!' he said. 'Dozens and hundreds of pairs o' boots. I feels that happy I don't care what I does.' Then, clasping a bottle-straw in each hand, he closed his eyes.

John and Susan went out of the cellar by the way they had come, and hurried back to breakfast.

A great many things had happened while they were away. A white hen that had laid astray and disappeared weeks ago had come clucking into the yard with a family of twelve late summer chickens. One of the kittens had fallen into a pan of cream and was being washed by its mother and scolded by Mrs Braithewaite. Lizzie had been stung by a wasp and Farmer Braithewaite had remembered that a man was coming to take the eggs into market and that they had not been collected yet. There was so much hustling and bustling going on that Gummidge's notice-board and the red handkerchiefs seemed to have been quite forgotten and no more questions were asked.

John and Susan helped to collect eggs from the hens' strange hiding-places in mangers, hayricks, hedges, and corners. Then they had a late breakfast and hurried back to Miss Duffy's house.

A second big furniture van was standing outside the gate. Its doors were open and it was half full of furniture. The children peeped inside because there is always something rather exciting about furniture that is not arranged dully on floors and round walls.

Evidently Miss Duffy was a careful person and had planned beforehand where each particular thing was to go. A label with the word 'kitchen' was fastened to the handle of a dresser, another, marked 'drawing-room', was tied to a table-leg.

But there was more than furniture in the van. Sticking out from between a wicker chair and a cupboard was the end of a ragged trouser leg, an inch or two of polished broomstick and a bottle-straw boot. Tied to the boot was a label which said 'potting-shed'.

'Gummidge,' said John. 'It must be Gummidge's leg. However did he tuck himself away in there?'

Susan didn't answer for a moment because she was staring at something in the far corner of the van. An ordinary person would have thought the something was a bundle of tarred string, but Susan had recognized Hannah Harrow's hair. It was lying in an untidy knot on a glass-topped table, but the rest of the scarecrow was hidden from sight.

'I hope she hasn't labelled herself "spare-bedroom" or "drawing-room" or any proper room,' said John.

'I wish we could get them out,' said Susan.

But it was too late, for there came a scrunching of feet on gravel and two furniture-removal men came back to the van to carry in more of Miss Duffy's possessions.

John and Susan moved out of the way and watched a glass fronted book-case being taken out of the van.

'Now's our chance,' said John as the book-case was being carried through the gates.

But the chance was gone because the washerwoman with two of her friends came walking down the road, and they too stopped to watch the carrying about of Miss Duffy's furniture.

'They say she's a very nice lady,' said the washer-woman, after the men had made three or four more journeys.

John and Susan hoped Miss Duffy was nice, when a wicker chair and a cupboard were pushed aside and one of the workmen looked down at the sulky form of Worzel Gummidge.

'Scarecrow, eh?' said one of them, 'that's a funny thing for an old lady to bring from London.'

'I didn't see it when we loaded up either,' said his companion. 'Still, if it says potting-shed, we'd better take it to the potting-shed.'

There was a creak and a rustle, as Worzel Gummidge was lifted out of the van and hauled by his stiff arms (while his head nodded and his straw heels brushed the gravel) up the drive and out of sight.

They would have liked to follow, but a rather cross-looking man in a white apron was standing on the front steps of the house, so they waited by the van.

The washerwoman and her friends walked on, but there was no chance of talking to Hannah Harrow or finding out if Earthy was in the van too because Tommy Higginsthwaite and about a dozen children came racing down the road and clustered round the van. They climbed inside it and began to finger the furniture until the man in the white apron came stumping down the drive and told them all to go away and scowled at Susan and John.

CHAPTER VIII

THE HANDY-MAN

—

THE next day was wet, so was the next, and so was the one after that. The holidays were very nearly at an end, and it seemed as if John and Susan would have no chance of seeing Worzel Gummidge. When, at last, the weather cleared up, they spent the greater part of their days in walking up and down past Miss Duffy's house. But the walls were high and the gates were solid. All they saw in the mornings was a housemaid shaking

mops and dusters from the upper windows. All they
saw in the afternoons were the old ladies of the village
going to call on Miss Duffy. Each one carried a card
case and an umbrella and each one closed the garden-
door behind her so quickly that it was impossible for
John or Susan to peep inside. Each old lady stayed for
about a quarter of an hour and when she left the garden
she shut the door again.

The children did wish that old ladies were not so
particular about shutting doors after them.

'It shows they've been well brought up,' said Susan.

'And it shows that it's a great mistake to bring people
up properly,' said John; 'I think it's very silly!'

They heard a good deal about Miss Duffy in the
village. People said she was very short-sighted and very
kind and very obstinate.

'She sounds a bit like Gummidge,' said Susan.

John argued that only the obstinate bit sounded like
Gummidge because he was neither short-sighted nor kind.

'He's fairly kind in some ways,' said Susan. 'You
couldn't expect anyone like Worzel Gummidge to go on
being kind all the time. He does lead such a difficult life.'

'He may be leading an easy one now,' said John. 'I do
wish we could find out. I could draw a map of that gate.'

It was about twelve o'clock and they happened to
have stopped outside Miss Duffy's house just in case they
could catch a glimpse of Worzel Gummidge.

'You can't draw maps of gates,' snapped Susan.

'I could of this one. I know every knot-hole and every
crack and every little dent and the pattern of the
hinges. And I don't care! I'm going to open the gate just
a chink.'

'You can't,' said Susan. 'Look, Mrs Higginsthwaite's
just coming down the road.'

Somebody always seemed to be coming down the road

at the wrong time. John and Susan wished Mrs Higginsthwaite would go away, especially when the latch of the
gate rattled and the gate itself began to open.

'If only that's Gummidge –' began Susan.

But it was not Gummidge. Tommy Higginsthwaite
came out of the garden, put his hands in his pockets, and
whistled the sort of tune that showed he was not feeling
so happy as he tried to sound.

'Well,' said Mrs Higginsthwaite from a few yards,
'Did you get the job as weeding-boy?'

'Miss Duffy says she's suited. She says she's got a man
and she doesn't want a boy.'

'That's only a tale,' said Mrs Higginsthwaite. 'She
hasn't got any man from hereabouts, that I do know.
And she didn't bring a man with her either – that I do
know, too.'

'That's what she said, anyway.' Tommy's voice was
sulky. 'And I saw a man too, a shabby-looking chap in
a black bowler hat.'

'I told you to wash your hands,' said Mrs Higginsthwaite.

Tommy scuffled up some dust, kicked a pebble along
the road and then turned to follow his mother back to
Scatterbrook.

'A black bowler hat,' repeated Susan five minutes later
when she and John had nearly reached the farm. 'A black
bowler hat. I wonder if it could be Gummidge.'

'We never shall know now,' grumbled John. 'We can't
know now because we're going home to-morrow.'

It was quite true. Mrs Braithewaite was busy packing
their big black trunk. Lizzie was ironing and folding
Susan's cotton frocks and John's shirts. Tickets had been
taken and the next day the fussy little train would carry
them far away from Scatterbrook.

Perhaps because she wanted to get them out of the

way while packing was going on, Mrs Braithewaite
told them that Miss Duffy had ordered a dozen eggs
which she wanted early in the afternoon, and she added
that John and Susan could take them to the White
House. She told them this at dinner-time.

Never had Mrs Braithewaite helped the pudding so
slowly. Never had golden syrup stuck so long to the
spoon as Susan tried to dollop it on to her plate. Never
had pudding been so hot when John tried to swallow it.
Never had a meal lasted so long.

And how slowly Mrs Braithewaite walked when she
went to find a basket for the eggs. How fussy she was
when she dusted it!

What difficult places the hens had hidden their eggs in!

At last eleven were found and then John and Susan
came face to face with an indignant-looking black hen
who was squatting in a manger.

'Oh! please say you've laid,' begged Susan. 'Please
don't keep us waiting.' She put out a hand and the black
hen pecked it quite hard.

'I'll soon see if she has laid,' said John, and he picked
up the hen with both hands.

There was a furious squawking, a struggle, and then
a flapping wing hit John in the eye. But the white egg
that the hen had left behind her was worth a sore finger
and a sore eye.

Five minutes later they were racing up the road that
led to the White House.

Sunblinds were drawn down behind every window,
a tabby cat was licking itself in the porch, but John
and Susan did not go to the front door because far away
to the right, beyond the croquet lawn and beyond the
asparagus bed, they had seen the familiar gawky form of
Hannah Harrow.

They dumped the eggs in the drive and ran across

the lawn. Hannah was wearing an old-fashioned sun-hat with a drooping straw brim.

'Hannah!' said Susan.

'Hannah!' said John.

Hannah Harrow did not answer, but somebody else did –

'She'll not speak till autumn now. She's gone back to her old work. Ooh aye! So's Earthy.'

There behind them stood Worzel Gummidge. He must have suddenly jerked himself up from among the goose-berry bushes. He had a hoe in his hand and he was wearing a green baize apron. Some bits of bast were wound round the crown of his old bowler.

'Whatever are you doing here?' asked John.

'Caretakin' same as I said I should. Me and Miss Duffy gets on fine together. She takes care o' me and I takes care o' the garden.'

'I don't think you are taking care of it very well,' remarked Susan, looking about her at the untidy veget-able plots. 'There are a frightful lot of weeds.'

'I takes care o' them too,' said Gummidge proudly. 'I never treads on 'em – not if I can help it and now and again I waters 'em.'

'But you shouldn't water *weeds*.'

'They gets thirsty same as everything else does,' said Gummidge. 'I takes care of the slugs too *and* the snails *and* the earwigs. When the slugs seems hungry I takes 'em over to the lettuces. Slugs like lettuces.'

'I don't call that taking care of the lettuces, though,' argued Susan.

'You can't take care of everything not all at the same time,' said Gummidge. 'When I wants to take care of the lettuces I moves the slugs back to the cabbages. They all gets their turns.'

Worzel Gummidge smiled happily as he creaked down-

wards and straightened a piece of groundsel which had
got bent.

'I caretakes like mad,' he muttered.

'Does Earthy help?' asked John.

'I told you Earthy's gone back to her old job of scaring.
So's Hannah. You'll find Earthy among the taters.'
Gummidge waved a hand towards a potato patch and
then continued to straighten some trampled weeds.

John and Susan had forgotten all about the eggs
because they were so interested in the ways of the three
scarecrows.

Gummidge did not seem inclined to talk any more,
so they left him and went in search of Earthy. They
found her, as he had told them, among the potatoes.
She had straddled her legs like a robin so that each foot
was planted in a ridge. The children noticed that somebody had earthed her feet up so that she looked as
though she had taken root. There was a pleasant smile
on her little brown face. Her arms stuck straight out
from her shoulders in the way that scarecrows usually
carry them when they are at work.

'Earthy!' said John.

'Earthy!' whispered Susan.

There was no answer and they found it difficult to
believe that this still and silent scarecrow had ever
bustled about among the fields and hedges.

Somebody spoke behind them, 'I see you are admiring
my scarecrows.'

It was Miss Duffy, a dear little old lady who wore a
shady straw hat and was raising a pair of lorgnettes to her
rather bird-like nose. 'I think I am very lucky to have
them. I have always been so fond of scarecrows.'

'Yes, so are we,' agreed Susan, and then John explained
who they were and why they had come, adding, 'We'd
better get the eggs for fear they get broken.'

On their way back to the lawn they passed Worzel Gummidge who was lolling against a gooseberry bush and had his eyes tightly shut.

'That is my handy-man,' explained Miss Duffy. 'Such a nice obliging man, but I am afraid he cannot be very strong. He often falls asleep in the middle of his work and does not wake up for hours.'

'Does – does he live in the house?' asked Susan.

'No, dear, in the potting-shed. He says he prefers it. I found him working in the garden the day I arrived – so kind of him, I thought. Really, I am very lucky to find somebody who really understands gardening because I know nothing about it. Do you?'

'Not – not very much,' answered Susan.

Miss Duffy went on happily.

'But ignorant as I am and short-sighted as I am, I can see that we have a very good show of – of – these flowers.'

With her ivory-handled stick, little Miss Duffy stroked a flourishing tuft of weeds.

'It is very foolish of me and they are so familiar, but I have quite forgotten the name of the flowers.'

'Groundsel,' said John in a choky voice.

'Yes, to be sure, to be sure. I am sure my groundsel is a credit to any gardener. I must congratulate my good Mr Gummidge as soon as he wakes up. Really he is a most painstaking man. It was he who set up those nice scarecrows in the garden. I don't know what I should do without him. And now shall we come into the house and see if we can find some chocolate biscuits?'

The children followed Miss Duffy into the house where they ate chocolate biscuits and sponge fingers and peppermint creams. While they were nibbling, Gummidge passed and re-passed the open window several times. They wondered what he was doing and when the plates were nearly empty and they themselves were nearly full they found out.

Miss Duffy walked down the drive with them and stopped to speak to Gummidge who was planting out some nettles between the rose bushes in a sunny border.

'Busy as usual,' she said.

'Ooh aye! And next year you'll have the best show of dandelions and buttercups in Scatterbrook. And the lawn will be white with daisies.'

Gummidge had kicked off one of his bottle-straw boots and was jabbing holes in the earth with the end of his leg.

'Such a hard worker,' murmured Miss Duffy as she moved off towards the gate.

Afterwards Susan and John wondered if they should have told her that Gummidge was really a scarecrow.

'I don't see why we should,' said Susan, 'after all *we* think dandelions are quite as pretty as marigolds.'

'And why shouldn't there be daisies on lawns?' said John. 'Ordinary plain grass is so dull.'

'Yes.' Susan licked a chocolate crumb from her lip. 'And it's lovely to think that Gummidge is being liked and looked after. It makes it much easier to go away from Scatterbrook.'

CHAPTER IX

GUMMIDGE GOES FISHING

—

JOHN and Susan had not expected to see Worzel Gummidge again for months and months. They thought that the autumn term would drag on as usual until the Christmas holidays; and that the holidays would race by,

that the weeks of the next term would seem like fort-
nights, and that they would have changed some of their
teeth and grown out of most of their clothes before they
met the scarecrows of Scatterbrook.

But, as it happened, only one of Susan's double teeth
had loosened and only last year's shoes were getting a
shade too tight for John before they were back at the
farm again.

The first reason was that they both went to the same
boarding-school for girls and boys. The second reason
was that fire broke out at the school and the most
important parts of the buildings were burned down.
(Nobody was hurt but everybody was sent home so that
the builders and decorators and carpenters could get on
with their work.) The third reason was that the parents
of John and Susan had shut up their house in London
and gone abroad for some months. So, of course, the
children went down to Scatterbrook.

The first thing they did, after all the greetings and un-
packings were over, was to ask after Miss Duffy.

'She,' said Mrs Braithewaite. 'Oh! she didn't stay
long. The White House is up for sale again. I shouldn't
think she'll sell it easily either because she let the garden
get into such a state.'

Susan glanced at John, but of course she couldn't say
anything just then. The news was not really surprising.
Somehow neither of the children had expected that
Gummidge would make a very successful gardener.

'It's a dreadful nuisance though!' said Susan. 'He may
have gone anywhere. We may never find him now.'

'I expect we shall,' said John. 'We always do, you know.'

It was too late to go out that afternoon, but the next
morning they went for a walk up to Ten-acre Field.

Now, just as they had not expected to see Gummidge
for months and months after they left Scatterbrook, so

they did not expect to find him for some days after their return. But then he was a very unexpected sort of scarecrow.

'Look!' said Susan when they had only walked halfway up the lane to Ten-acre Field. 'Look, there he is.'

The scarecrow was leaning against a gateway that led to Ten-acre Field, and he did not look at all surprised when the children said, 'Good morning.'

'Mornin',' he answered in a sulky voice.

'We've come back,' said John.

'Ooh aye!'

It was rather a depressing sort of greeting, so Susan began to ask questions about his gardening and about Miss Duffy.

'Her and me fell out,' Gummidge told her. 'She would keep opening the front door after I'd nailed up some bindweed across it. Obstinate, she were, so I come away. "Grow your own nettles!" I says and I fell into a sulk.'

Gummidge looked so sulky as he spoke that John asked, 'How's Earthy?'

'Wet!' was the answer. 'Soakin' wet!'

'But it isn't raining,' said Susan in a very surprised voice. 'There hasn't been any rain for simply ages.'

'That's what she says,' agreed Gummidge.

He clung to one of the bars of the gate, raised both his legs until they were sticking straight out in front of him, let go of the gate and sat down with a plop.

'That's what she says,' he repeated, and a pained expression came over his turnipy face, for he really had sat down very hard and very suddenly. 'That's what she says, and that's why she's having a washing-day. I've tried argufying, I've tried scolding and I've tried sulking. The last thing I said before I sulked was that there's no sense in tampering with Nature. "If you was meant to be washed," I said, "and if your clothes was meant to be washed, then there'd be a nice shower. There'll be rain enough in the winter," I said. "Take a holiday while you can." After that I started on a real good sulk. And what do you think she did to me then?'

'What did she do?' asked Susan.

Gummidge frowned terribly as he answered, 'She came and sat on my knee and put her arms round my neck. Ugh!' He gave a sort of shiver. At least the children supposed it was a shiver. He shook himself for some time until his straw stuffing rustled and his broomstick legs clattered together.

'How very sweet of her,' said Susan.

Gummidge shuddered again. 'She hugged me,' he complained, 'and the water ran out of her sleeves and began trickling down my neck. Then she began to wring her skirt out all over my trousers. Spoiled my sulk, spoiled my trousers, spoiled my day!'

'But do you mean that she'd been washing her clothes when they were *on* her?' asked John.

'No sense in takin' 'em off, is there?' snapped Gummidge. 'Earthy may be soft but she's not daft yet. She never was one to waste time. I can see her now getting out of that cattle-trough. "Enough to turn you mouldy!" I said. "I don't want a mildewed wife." She's drying off now.'

'And what are you doing?' asked Susan.

Gummidge sighed a gusty sigh.

'Restin',' he answered. 'I'm fair wore out with chasin' after clothes.'

'What *do* you mean?' asked John.

Gummidge suddenly looked alarmingly sulky, and Susan whispered to John, 'I don't think we'd better ask many questions while he's so cross.'

However the scarecrow answered sullenly:

'I means what I says. It's like this – Earthy, *she* said

that if I didn't get clean clothes she'd wash mine and me in 'em. So here I sits waitin' for the clothes.'

Suddenly a very curious sound came from behind a haystack in the small field.

'What's that?' asked John. 'Pigs?'

Gummidge smiled for the first time that morning and stood up in a creaky way.

'That's what I've been waitin' for,' he said, 'waitin' and hopin' for. But maybe we'd better give him a minute or two longer.'

'Give who a minute or two longer?' asked Susan. 'I do wish you'd explain.'

'I am explaining,' said Gummidge. 'I told you I've been following clothes about half the mornin'. *Occupied* clothes too – clothes that's inhabited by someone that walks fast. Come on now. I'm not going to wait no longer.'

Gummidge raised the latch of the gate with his twiggy fingers, pushed it open, and began to walk sideways into the field. The children followed as he shuffled round the haystack. Then he put a finger to his lips and gave a sort of jerk of the other hand to beckon them on.

There lying on his back and fast asleep was a tramp. His cap was over his eyes and he was snoring loudly. By his side was a pair of boots. Gummidge grabbed these and led the way back to the lane.

'Selfish thing,' he muttered. 'He might have took off his coat as well.'

'But you aren't going to steal them, are you?' asked Susan in a shocked voice.

For answer Gummidge took off first one bottle-straw boot and then another and tossed them in the direction of the haystack.

'Exchange ain't no robbery!' he said. 'That's wrote down in a book somewhere so it must be true. These boots is nearly new, but then o' course boots is always easy to come by. Tramps cast 'em just as snakes cast their skin. Trousers is difficult – they take on an' off so awkward, that's what it is.'

While he was talking, Worzel Gummidge was snatching handfuls of grass and clover from the side of the road and stuffing them into his boots.

'Lucky he's got small feet,' he remarked, 'it saves a lot of work.'

After he had put on the boots he stood up.

'Well, I'll have to be getting on,' he said. 'Pity you're such dwarfs or I could have had some of the clothes off of you.'

'We aren't dwarfs,' said Susan indignantly. 'Everyone says that I'm very well grown for my age. So is John.'

'I don't believe in changing every year myself,' said Gummidge. 'Look at you now – the older you get the further you've got to stoop every time you do a shoelace up. 'Tain't fair; you don't get a chance of getting used to yourselves. Now I'm only six inches shorter since the day I was made.'

'Why *shorter?*' asked Susan. 'We grow *bigger.*'

'I said shorter,' replied Gummidge, 'and I means shorter. It happened about five years ago. A man sawed a bit off my leg and whittled it down to make one of those things for dibbling in turnips. Then it split, and it were lucky it did or I might have walked lame for the rest of my life. After that he lopped off six inches from the other leg.'

'But didn't it hurt?' asked Susan.

'We scarecrows haven't got touchy feelings like that,' answered Gummidge proudly. 'It were a bit awkward in one way though because my trousers were tight under the arm already and they couldn't be hitched no higher. They got a bit muddy and frayed but nothing to worry about. Well, I'll have to go on chasing clothes. Good morning!'

Gummidge took off his hat, tossed it up in the air, caught it and put it on his head again.

'He is getting polite, isn't he?' said Susan when they were out of hearing. 'He never did that when we first knew him.'

They went back to lunch after that, because they knew that Mrs Braithewaite, the farmer's wife, was giving them Norfolk dumplings and a treacle tart and it would never do to be late.

Directly the meal was over they scuttled out of the house because they did so want to find Worzel Gummidge again.

But though they went up to Ten-acre Field and into the little spinney and up to the Downs, they saw no sign of the scarecrow, and it was nearly tea-time when they returned to Scatterbrook village.

'There's a tea-party somewhere,' said Susan.

'How do you know?' asked John.

'Because I've seen so many old ladies in gloves and best hats,' was the answer. 'And they are all going towards the vicarage and –'

'Ow!' said John and his hand swept up towards his hair.

'OW!' he repeated, this time more loudly.

'What's the matter?' asked Susan.

'Wasp or something. It stung me!' John rubbed his forehead under the tuft of thick hair in front and then sucked his finger.

Before Susan could answer they both heard a sheep-like cough. It came from the walnut tree just above them.

'Sorry!' said the voice of Worzel Gummidge. 'You'd best come up here if you don't want to be hurt. I never was much good at fishin'.'

Susan and John looked up and there, hidden among the glossy leaves of the walnut tree, they saw something

which anybody else might have mistaken for an old
turnip half-covered by a bowler hat.

'It's Gummidge!' said Susan.

'Of course it's Gummidge!' wheezed a familiar voice.
'Who else would it be? Are you coming up or aren't you?'

They went up the tree. Luckily a grey stone wall
helped them in their climb. Two minutes later they too
were hidden among the green and were perched astride
of a big branch while Worzel Gummidge tried to
disentangle a fish-hook from his hat while he muttered
to himself:

'No, I never was much good at fishin' nor at catchin'
what I want. I've hooked a perambulator and a hoop
and some straw that was having a ride on a cart, but I've
not caught any clothes yet.'

'Are you really fishing for clothes?' whispered Susan.

'Ooh aye, of course I am. Don't talk so loud now:
she's coming.'

'Who's coming?' asked John

'That woman that dresses up like a daft bird and wears
feathers on her head,' answered Gummidge.

Susan and John peeped down through the leaves of the
walnut tree. There, mincing along the village street and
wearing very high-heeled shoes, came Mrs Bloomsbury-
Barton. On her head was a purple velvet hat. On the hat
were some pale-grey ostrich feathers.

'It's not what I'd have chosen,' muttered Gummidge
as he freed the hook and sent it quivering down on the
end of his line, 'But scarecrows can't be choosers.'

'Oughtn't you to have baited the hook?' whispered
John.

Mrs Bloomsbury-Barton had stopped to talk to a
woman, who was wheeling a perambulator, so there was
plenty of time for the question.

'Maybe,' said Gummidge as he paid out more line.

'Maybe I should, but what would you bait it with?
'Tisn't likely she eats flies nor worms neither and I'm
not going to spend money on bits of meat or fish or cheese
or bird-seed neither.'

'But she isn't a bird,' giggled Susan.

'Then what does she want to wear feathers on her head
for?' asked Gummidge fiercely. ''Tain't natural if she
isn't a bird. Hush!'

Mrs Bloomsbury-Barton, who had finished talking,
was hurrying towards the walnut tree. Lower and lower
dangled Gummidge's hook. It swung once above the
hat, then two inches lower and at last it caught in one
of the velvet folds. Up went the hat on the end of the
line. Up went Mrs Bloomsbury-Barton's hands, but they
only clutched at air.

'Oh!' breathed John.

'Oh!' sighed Susan in a horrified whisper. 'She's got
black hair, and I always thought it was red.'

The next moment Gummidge's bowler hat had
whizzed down into the road about three feet in front of
Mrs Bloomsbury-Barton.

'Exchange ain't no robbery!' he wheezed for the
second time that day.

Mrs Bloomsbury-Barton looked up. Unfortunately
Gummidge was so well hidden by leaves that she saw
only John and Susan at first.

'You disgracefully impertinent little boy,' she said.
'Give me back my hat at once and my – my – that is
to say my other property.'

'But it wasn't John,' said Susan, 'really it wasn't.'

Mrs Bloomsbury-Barton snatched at a purple silk scarf
she was wearing and draped it over her curious stubbly-
looking black hair. Then she spoke to Susan.

'Unless you give me back my hat at once,' she said,
'I shall – I shall –'

Gummidge wriggled his way slowly along the thick branch of the tree. In one hand he held the purple velvet hat and in another Mrs Bloomsbury-Barton's red wig.

'Oh!' said Susan, who now understood the reason of Mrs Bloomsbury-Barton's black hair.

'Been birds-nestin' have you?' he said. 'Birds-nestin's a thing that ought to be stopped.'

'Hush!' said Susan, in a whisper. 'That isn't a bird's nest. It's her wig!'

'Earwig!' croaked Gummidge. 'Earwig indeed! Earwigs don't build nests. I tell you it's a bird's nest.'

'Will you please give me my hat and other property at once,' said Mrs Bloomsbury-Barton angrily.

For answer Gummidge put the purple velvet hat on to his own head.

'Does it suit me?' he asked anxiously.

Nobody answered him. John, Susan, and Mrs Bloomsbury-Barton were all looking along the road. A policeman wheeling his bicycle, two or three school-children and the Vicar's wife were all coming towards the walnut tree. Mrs Bloomsbury-Barton gave a little shudder.

'You may well shiver,' said Gummidge fiercely. 'Ooh aye! You may well look scared. Just you wait till I've showed this nest to the policeman and see what he'll have to say to you.' He tilted the velvet hat at a sharper angle on his head and went on. 'I knows the policeman and I knows what he thinks of birds-nesting. Why, there was a boy once in Scatterbrook that took a goldfinch's nest and you've never heard such a to-do.'

Mrs Bloomsbury-Barton gave a curious little bleating sound, for the Vicar's wife and the children were coming nearer and she did not want anyone to know about her red wig.

'It isn't a bird's nest,' said Susan. 'Do give it back to her.'

'Wild Birds' Protection Act,' scolded Gummidge. 'There's a notice about that outside the police station. I don't know what sort of a bird made this nest but it must have been wild enough to choose a colour like that. Took a lot of pains too, poor thing, and then you go and rob it!'

Nearer and nearer came the policeman. Mrs Bloomsbury-Barton opened her mouth and shut it again. Just at that moment a puff of wind lifted the hat from Gummidge's head. Mrs Bloomsbury-Barton grabbed it as it fell, rammed it on to her head and hurried down the road in the direction of her own house.

'And never a word of thanks,' said Gummidge sadly as he wriggled his way backwards into the shadow of the leaves.

'I shouldn't really talk about birds-nesting to the policeman, if I were you,' said John, 'because –'

'Nor shall I, as I *am* me,' agreed Gummidge. 'He might want his pyjamas back. I'm generally lucky on other people's washing days.' He patted a pink and white bundle that was rolled up in the crook of a branch.

'Oh!' said Susan. 'Did you really steal the policeman's pyjamas off the clothes line?'

'Didn't steal!' said Gummidge. 'He can have my suit when I've had time to change.'

'Do you think he'll want it?' asked John.

'Couldn't say I'm sure,' said Gummidge carelessly. 'That's not my business.' Then he added: 'Well, I suppose if she can wear a nest on her head I can. The bird must be tired of lookin' for it by now.' He fitted the red wig over his turnipy head and smiled genially.

'Suit me?' he asked.

'No, it doesn't,' said John crossly. 'And I expect you've got us into an awful row. Come on, Susan.'

When they were in the road again Gummidge leaned

out of the tree to wave to them. In the red wig, he looked more peculiar than ever.

'There won't be no row,' he said. 'She won't want anyone else in Scatterbrook to know she goes birds-nestin'.'

As a matter of fact, Gummidge was right. Late that evening when John and Susan were returning from a walk on the Downs, Mrs Bloomsbury-Barton walked down to her garden gate and beckoned to them. In one hand she carried a box of chocolates.

'Good evening, dears,' she said. 'I wonder do you like chocolates?'

John and Susan gaped at her, and she continued. 'I think we had better let bygones be bygones. Supposing we all agree to say nothing to anyone about that little practical joke of this afternoon. Wouldn't that be a good idea?'

Before John or Susan could answer they were startled by the sound of a familiar cough. Somebody wearing pink pyjamas and an old bowler hat moved creakily from behind a lilac tree just inside the gate.

'What did I tell you!' said Gummidge. 'She doesn't want anyone to know about the birds-nestin'!'

He handed a limp-looking red wig to Mrs Bloomsbury-Barton.

'You can have it back,' he said. 'Earthy says it don't suit me. It does seem a pity! Good evenin'.'

CHAPTER X

THE ENTERTAINMENT

—

IT was a dismal morning and John and Susan were awakened by the sound of rain beating against the

windows of their bedrooms. The farm-yard was full
of puddles and there was very little answer to Mrs
Braithewaite's cries of 'chick-chick-chick' when she went
out to feed the hens. The fowls shook their wet feathers
angrily and pecked at their food in a dismal sort of
way. Only the ducks seemed happy and far more talk-
ative than usual.

Mrs Braithewaite was in a bad temper, and snapped
at her husband when he came tramping into the kitchen
just after breakfast.

'Come in now, do, and shut the door. I don't want
the cat to get at the ducklings.'

The farmer banged the door in a way that John and
Susan envied; and he stamped first one boot and then
another on the red brick floor in a way that they envied too.

'If the cat was the only trouble I'd think life was
easy,' he answered, as the studs of his boots rang on the
floor again so that dollops of mud were scattered.

'Whatever's the matter with *you* this morning?' asked
Mrs Braithewaite.

'The roof of the village hall's leaking.'

'It always does.'

'Land's sake!' snapped the farmer, 'Don't you remember it's the day of the village concert and I was fool
enough to tell Mrs Bloomsbury-Barton that if it rained
to-day they could use our big loft.'

'It'll mean a lot of work,' complained Mrs Braithewaite as she put bacon and eggs on to her husband's
plate. 'Whatever made you promise such a silly thing?'

'Because I thought it would be fine,' said the farmer.
'I'm seldom wrong as a weather prophet.'

'Well, it never rains but it pours,' said Mrs Braithewaite.

'I'm rather glad it's raining,' whispered Susan to
John. 'We'll have a lovely cobwebby morning helping

to clear out the loft. And we'll have front row seats because we'll be there first.'

But as it happened they did not have a lovely cobwebby morning, because everything went wrong. The first thing to happen was that Mrs Braithewaite saw that the key of the little loft was missing from its hook, and the little loft had been promised by the farmer as a dressing-room for the performers at the concert.

They all looked for the key in every possible place – under the mats, behind the clock and even in the oven until they were quite hot and almost breathless.

Then by the time they had decided that the little loft couldn't be used, Mrs Bloomsbury-Barton came click-clicking up the flagged path, and after she had talked for a little with Mrs Braithewaite she turned to the children.

'Good morning, Susan, dear. Good morning, John. I am sure you are both longing to help with the preparations for the concert. I have some quite important work for you to do. We are short of programmes so I want some more copied out. Now which of you is the neatest writer?'

'John,' said Susan.

'Susan,' said John.

They both spoke so quickly that the answer sounded like *Johnsan*, but Mrs Bloomsbury-Barton seemed to understand.

'I am sure you both write *beautifully!*' she said. 'Shall we say a dozen copies each? That will be *splendid!*'

'But –' began Susan. 'But we're rather specially busy this morning. We promised Farmer Braithewaite that we would help in the loft this morning, didn't we, Mrs Braithewaite?'

Now ordinarily Mrs Braithewaite might have been helpful, but to-day she wasn't because she was feeling cross.

'I don't know what *you* promised, but I do know *he* won't want you messing about with brooms and getting under everybody's feet.'

John and Susan both went rather red because they didn't like being talked about as though they were kittens or ducklings.

'What about our walk?' asked John earnestly. 'You know we're supposed to go for a walk every morning, don't you, Mrs Braithewaite?'

'Yes, you know we are,' said Susan. 'You always say it's so good for us!'

Mrs Braithewaite glanced at the rain-blurred window. 'Walk indeed, and in rain like this! I never heard such an idea.'

Mrs Bloomsbury-Barton beamed at everybody, and handed a programme to John and another to Susan.

'So that's all beautifully settled,' she said. 'And now I must simply *fly*. Good-bye, children. Good-bye, Mrs Braithewaite, I shall be back soon.'

So John got ink on his fingers instead of cobwebs in his hair; and Susan sucked her pen instead of nibbling at the apples which were always stored in the barn until apples were ripe on the trees.

The programme did not look particularly interesting while they were making the first copy. By the time John had reached his tenth and Susan her eleventh, it seemed to be the dullest thing they had ever read. There was only one exciting line on the whole page and that was: 'Surprise Item, arranged by Mrs Bloomsbury-Barton.' It was due to begin just after the interval.

'All the same,' said John, 'all the same, if it has anything to do with Mrs Bloomsbury-Barton, it's certain to be dull.'

'Still a surprise *is* a surprise, and surprises are generally fun,' said Susan, mumbling rather because she hadn't quite finished drawing a red ink moustache on her lip.

Her words turned out to be truer than either of them had expected. Certainly the concert was rather dull to begin with. The most exciting thing about it was that it was being held in the big hay-loft instead of in the village hall. Hurricane lanterns, which had been slung from the beams, lit up the cobwebs and threw queer shadows on to the walls.

Every now and then the mooing of a cow from one of the stalls below mixed rather queerly with the nervous voices of the singers.

The piano seemed to upset the roosters, so really it was rather a good thing when the curtain was dropped for the interval and everybody went to the far end of the loft for refreshments.

'It's the surprise item next,' remarked John. 'I wonder what it will be.'

'Something to do with the school-children I think,' said Susan. 'They've all disappeared.'

Mrs Bloomsbury-Barton overheard her.

'You must not even *try* to guess,' she said. 'It must be a real surprise. And now I must *skip* across to the farm and put the finishing touch to somebody's costume. It is *so* unfortunate that we aren't able to use the small loft as a dressing-room.'

Long before everybody had had their second cups of tea and while Mrs Braithewaite was still turning the tap of the great urn on and off and trying in between times to see that there was plenty of milk and sugar, there was a strange thumping and bumping noise. It seemed to come from behind the stage curtain, and was so loud that everyone looked up. The thumpings and scrapings and bangings grew louder than ever. Then the curtain bulged, and at least half the notes on the piano were all played at once.

'The surprise item I shouldn't wonder,' remarked Mrs Braithewaite, and when they heard all the mothers of the village made a rush for the front seats. Other people crowded into the back ones, and only just in time too because the stage curtain was going up in an uncertain and jerky way. When it was about eighteen inches from the floor it stopped suddenly. From beneath it could be seen a very curious collection of legs, boots, and sticks. Somebody began to play the piano, or rather one note of it, in a fitful sort of way. 'I'm sure Gummidge is behind the curtain,' whispered Susan to John. 'I'd know his boots anywhere. And those are Upsidaisy's three legs.'

'They *may* be the legs of a milking-stool,' replied John doubtfully, 'I mean the legs of a milking-stool that doesn't belong to Upsidaisy.'

The monotonous tinkling of the piano went on until the audience began to shuffle feet and cough, and then to clap and stamp and scrape chairs backwards and forwards. The people made so much noise that the strange sounds that came drifting from behind the curtain could scarcely be heard at first. Farmer Braithewaite was the first to notice them.

'Sounds as though our old cow's took bad,' he said.

'Hush!' said somebody else. 'They're beginning to sing now.' Certainly, whoever were on the stage were making sounds now that might possibly be mistaken for singing. There was a shrill voice and a husky one, a quavering voice and a bellowing one, a voice that sounded like a gate creaking on rusty hinges and a voice that resembled corncrakes. At first all the voices seemed to be singing different words on different notes, but after a time it became clear that some sort of chorus was being attempted. John and Susan could distinguish Gummidge's voice and those of his friends as they sang –

'*Us be scarecrows, yes we be,*
    Bearing our banner,
Held up by Earthy who's married to me,
    Assisted by Hannah.

And we're all on strike together, you see,
    And come to this party.
Who's that singing like a rusty key?
    "*Oh! my name is Clarty.*"

An' we all had a meeting and put to the vote
    So don't think we're crazy
That we all wants boots and a brolly and a coat –'

Here was a pause and then the line was repeated in a hesitating sort of way –

'*That we all wants boots and a brolly and a coat –*'

Then a squeaky little voice finished –

'*And a kiss for Upsidaisy.*'

'A kiss for Earthy Mangold, you mean!' shouted Gummidge angrily. There was no mistaking his voice as he sang alone –

'*You won't calm me with a cast-off clout*
    And wore-out rubbige,
I'll sulk and sulk till my sulks wears out,
    I'm Worzel Gummidge.'

Susan clutched John by the arm because she was so anxious about what might happen next.

'What a very remarkable performance,' remarked the Vicar. 'Most original, but I wish they'd raise the curtain and let us see what it is all about. I really –'

But before he could finish his sentence the curtain began to go up in slow jerks.

There were seven scarecrows on the stage. One of

them (who wore a placard with the words 'No Hawkers' printed on it) stood with its back to the audience and continued to rap out its melancholy one-fingered, one-noted tune. Hannah Harrow was standing on a little heap of sawdust just behind the footlights. She was wearing her sacking dress and was hatless. Her tarred string hair had been twisted into two even lengths of rope; one of these was decorated with a few hen feathers and the other was tied with a bow of gardening bast.

Gummidge, wearing an enormous pair of pink pyjamas and his usual hat, stood glaring savagely at the audience. The three-legged scarecrow whose name was Upsidaisy was dressed in a sailor hat, green velveteen coat and a kilt which was short enough to show his three milking-stool legs. Earthy was smiling at everyone and Clarty was pushing back his newspaper stuffing in a moody sort of way. Gummidge's nephew was sitting on the piano and flapping his fly-swatter hands.

As the audience clapped all the scarecrows bowed as well as they could, though not very gracefully, and Worzel Gummidge gave Hannah a prod.

'Sing your piece!' he ordered.

A slow green blush spread over Hannah Harrow's turnip face.

'I'm that shy!' she simpered.

'This ain't no place for shyness, this ain't,' said Gummidge. Hannah Harrow stepped forward, scattering more sawdust on to the floor. Then she sang in a shrill mouse-like squeak –

> *'I'm little Hannah Harrow,*
> *I'm as shabby as a sparrow,*
> *But I've always done my duty by the crops.'*

As she finished she covered her face with her hands

and Upsidaisy trundled towards the footlights and
finished the verse:

> *'I'm little Upsidaisy*
> *And I never have been lazy*
> *But I've wore my stockings out except the tops –'*

As he sang the last line Upsidaisy pulled up his kilt
and showed two brown sock-tops and one navy blue
one. Two of his legs were quite smooth and polished
but one was rather badly splintered. He had one white
canvas shoe, one brown leather sandal and one black
boot, and they all varied in size.

The audience cheered loudly especially when Upsidaisy dropped his kilt and said:

'Still, it don't do to grumble. I've a lot to be thankful for!'

'However did they get the children up to look like
that?' asked Mrs Kibbins.

'Oh!' said her neighbour, 'that one perched on the
milking stool will be Mrs Turnpike's Maud – a perfect
little actress she is.'

'Mrs Turnpike's Maud indeed,' sniffed Mrs Kibbins.
'If you ask me, I don't believe it's children at all: more
likely a company hired from London.'

'Yes, yes,' agreed the Vicar. 'I can hardly believe that
these are amateur actors. I seem to have seen that tall
fellow before – probably on the London stage.'

Then while Mrs Braithewaite said that the tall one
nearly made her die of laughing and Mrs Kibbins agreed
that she had never seen such a comical face, Gummidge
stepped forward and began to wave his arms just as he
used to do when he was scaring the rooks in Ten-acre
Field.

'Ladies and Gentlemen,' he said. 'This here's a strike.
What we wants is your clothes so as we can give the rooks
a good scare –'

The audience laughed happily.

'That one will be the death of me!' said Mrs Kibbins. 'Did ever you think folks could get themselves up to look as like scarecrows as these do?'

'It's wonderful what they can do on the stage nowadays,' said Mrs Braithewaite.

'There ain't nothing to laugh at,' continued Worzel Gummidge. 'This here's a strike. Ooh aye! Us scarecrows know all about strikes. We all read the papers when they blows our way.' The little voice of Upsidaisy interrupted, 'I never read a paper but once and that was a paper bag – the writing on it was all about toffee. Still it don't do to grumble.'

Upsidaisy smiled happily, but Gummidge scowled.

'It's me what's making this speech. You give over talkin' and show 'em your stockings again.'

'There's not much to show,' objected Upsidaisy. 'There's nothing left of 'em now except the tops. They wore out all the way up. But it's no use frettin'. Many a poor scarecrow's only got a garter and that so stretched it's got to be worn round the middle. But it don't do to grumble.'

As soon as Upsidaisy stopped talking, the audience began to clap, and Mrs Braithewaite said – 'Such a tiny mite too! How she manages to keep her balance on that milking-stool fair beats me.'

The clapping seemed to please Upsidaisy, who trundled his way towards the footlights, and repeated, 'It don't do to grumble, do it?'

'It *do* do to grumble!' shouted Gummidge furiously. 'Ooh aye – that's what we're here for. We've come here to grumble and strike and sulk.'

He shambled slowly forward towards the row of hurricane lanterns which took the place of footlights. The lanterns hanging from the rafters of the loft had been turned down very low, and the figures of the scarecrows made strange shadows on the white-washed wall behind them.

Nobody said a word as Worzel Gummidge stumbled into one of the footlights and nearly overbalanced. Then one of his broomstick legs became entangled with the cords of the curtain. He looked at it furiously, sat down with his usual suddenness and the curtain came down with a rush.

Strange scufflings and rustlings could be heard from behind it, and the sound of scarecrow's feet shuffling across the stage. But the curtain remained down while the audience began to clap and stamp and shout.

'You'd almost think they were real scarecrows,' said Mrs Braithewaite when everybody's hands were tingling from clapping.

'I hope they're going to put on another turn,' said somebody else.

John and Susan did not speak at all: they were much too anxious to know what Worzel Gummidge was going to do next.

The curtain stayed down for so long that people began to look at one another in an enquiring way.

'Maybe they can't get the curtain up,' suggested Mrs Braithewaite.

'That's what the trouble is,' agreed Mrs Kibbins, 'the curtain's stuck, tricky things curtains are.'

'Perhaps we had better see what has occurred,' said the Vicar. 'Possibly there is some little hitch. A pity – great pity after such an excellent performance.'

So the Vicar, followed by Mr Braithewaite, walked towards the stage, climbed over the footlights and disappeared behind the curtain.

Susan clutched John's arm and they both kept quite

still as slowly, terribly slowly it seemed to them, the curtain went up foot by foot.

Except for Farmer Braithewaite and the Vicar there was nobody on the stage at all. Only a piece of turnip, a little heap of sawdust and something that looked like a strand of Hannah Harrow's tarred hair remained to show that the scarecrows had ever been there at all.

The Vicar cleared his throat, stepped to the front of the stage and announced that he would give a recitation.

John and Susan waited a second or two, then they tip-toed softly out of the loft, closing the door behind them. They did not speak a word until they were at the foot of the sloping stairway when Susan said, 'Where can they have gone? Oh! I do wish they wouldn't try to get mixed up with grown-up people. They always make trouble.'

'I thought it was fun,' said John, 'and nobody knew that they *were* scarecrows.'

'They're bound to find out,' Susan's voice was gloomy. 'Oh! listen! What's that noise?'

'Only somebody dancing on the stage, I should think,' said John.

But the sound did not come from the stage; it came from a disused cow-shed; so John and Susan tip-toed across the muddy yard to find out what was happening. They were puzzled to see that there was a light in the shed.

When John and Susan were half way across the yard, they heard a familiar cough, and saw Worzel Gummidge shuffling through the lighted doorway. He had put on his usual clothes over his pink pyjamas. They could see this because the pyjama trousers were longer than his own and hung down over his boots. The children followed him and then, in the light of the great stable lantern, they saw a strange sight.

Huddled up in an iron manger in the corner was Mrs Bloomsbury-Barton. Below her was Farmer Braithewaite's large fierce billy-goat which had, as the frayed rope on its collar showed, broken away from its pen. Sometimes the goat danced, sometimes it lowered its head and charged at a sheep hurdle below the manger. It was not a very good-tempered creature and Susan was afraid of it, so she clutched John by the arm and dragged him in the shadows.

'There you go,' said Gummidge, 'at it again!'

'Please, please take this dreadful creature away,' begged Mrs Bloomsbury-Barton.

'Ooh aye!' said Gummidge, 'I've caught you at it again.' John and Susan thought that he must be addressing the goat until he added, 'First you goes birds-nesting and then you goes tormentin' poor animals that have never done you any harm.'

It looked to John and Susan as though the goat would be far more likely to do Mrs Bloomsbury-Barton harm. It began to dance in quite a frenzied way. Its sharp hooves made clickety noises on the floor of the shed.

'What do you want to go teasing goats for?' asked Gummidge.

'I am not teasing the creature.'

'Tantalizin' then.' Gummidge moved sideways as the goat tried to butt him. 'If jumpin' up out of reach of a poor goat ain't teasin' and tantalizin' I don't know what is. Downright cruel, I calls it.'

'My good man –' began Mrs Bloomsbury-Barton.

'That's where you're wrong,' answered Gummidge rudely, 'that shows you don't understand nothing about anything. I'm not yours, I'm my own. I'm not good, I'm just fair to middlin' and I'm not a man – I'm a scarecrow.'

'Oh dear!' said Mrs Bloomsbury-Barton, and she

sounded so distressed that John and Susan felt quite sorry for her. '*Please* take this goat away.'

An obstinate expression came over Gummidge's face as he answered, 'I never were one to interfere with poor animals havin' a bit o' fun. That goat's enjoying itself. Ooh aye! And it leads a dull life, poor creature!'

All the same, the goat did not seem to be leading at all a dull life. It capered and pranced. Sometimes it butted Gummidge in the middle. Every time it did this he rustled a little, but otherwise he took no more notice than if he had been a stook of straw.

'Take it away! Take it away!' said Mrs Bloomsbury-Barton.

'That's just what I shall do,' said Gummidge, 'I'm not going to leave the poor thing to be teased by you any longer.'

He shambled out of the shed and the goat followed him. John and Susan followed too, for somehow they knew that Gummidge would never let the goat hurt them. They kept well in the shadows until they were out of the farm-yard.

'You *are* naughty,' said Susan as various scufflings and tappings told that Mrs Bloomsbury-Barton was getting down from the manger.

'It were a good entertainment,' said Gummidge. 'Better than what hers will be. Now weren't it a good entertainment?'

'Well, yes,' said John.

'Where are all the others?' asked Susan.

'Gone home long ago. You can have the key of the little loft now if you likes. We've finished with it.'

Gummidge took a rather muddy key from his pocket.

'Good evenin'!' he said, and walked down the road followed by the goat.

Mrs Bloomsbury-Barton was being congratulated

by everybody when John and Susan went back to
the big loft, but she seemed to be too puzzled and
flustered to make any sensible reply, which was really
just as well.

CHAPTER XI

GUY AND GUMMIDGE

—

IT was the fourth of November, a dark crisp evening and
there was a smell of turnips in the air that reminded
John and Susan of Worzel Gummidge. They were on
their way to the village shop to buy fireworks for the
next day's bonfire. Really, they ought to have bought
them in the morning, but there is something exciting
about shopping at night, so Mrs Braithewaite had lent
them a hurricane lantern and told them not to stay out
too late.

The rustling of leaves as they shuffled their way under
the beech trees reminded them of the sounds made by
Gummidge's bottle-straw boots, and their own shadows
looked like long and leggy scarecrows too.

'What's that?' asked Susan suddenly.

'What's what?' John swung the lantern so suddenly
that the shadows stretched out like elastic and then
shrank again.

'That squeaky noise.'

'It's only somebody pushing a pram.'

It was somebody pushing a pram: the squeaking
stopped just outside Mrs Kibbins' cottage and a worse
noise took its place.

'Penny for the Guy! Penny for the Guy! Who'll give
a penny for the old Guy,' shouted Tommy Higginsthwaite, and then he began to sing –

'Please to remember
The Fifth of November,
The Gunpowder Treason and plot,
I see no reason why Gunpowder Treason
Should ever be forgot.'

John and Susan stopped shuffling through the leaves and tip-toed towards the cottage. They were just in time to see Tommy Higginsthwaite leave the go-cart (for it wasn't a pram after all) and run up the garden path. They heard a knock at the door and a moment later Mrs Kibbins' whiney voice complaining that she hadn't any pennies to spare and wouldn't waste them on Guys if she had. Then she added that Tommy Higginsthwaite could have some new scones if he liked though he didn't deserve them.

Then the door shut and John and Susan were alone in the road. At least they thought they were alone until they were startled by the familiar cough they had heard so often.

'It's Gummidge!' said Susan. 'It must be Gummidge. Nobody else coughs like that.'

'But where is he?'

'In the go-cart, silly. I expect Gummidge was sulking and Tommy Higginsthwaite mistook him for Guy Fawkes.'

But the limp figure in the go-cart did not look like Worzel Gummidge. To begin with its hat was different and was pulled right down over its face.

'There!' said John. 'I'll show you it isn't Worzel Gummidge.' He pulled off the hat while Susan gave a little shiver because it seemed such a rude thing to do. A second later she was shouting 'Gummidge! Gummidge! Worzel Gummidge, what are you doing?'

'Shut up!' said John. 'We don't want Tommy to come out.'

Worzel Gummidge looked sulkier than ever. His green tufts of hair sprouted untidily all over his turnipy head and his eyes were tightly shut as they always were when he was angry.

He did not open them until John and Susan had spoken to him at least six times. Then he said in his crossest voice:

'I'm not Worzel Gummidge – so there!'

'Of course you're Gummidge,' said John.

'And I tells you I'm not. I'm the one to know who I am, aren't I? I'm not Gummidge, I'm Guy. Mr Guy Fawkes – that's my name. They've made me a bonfire and I'm going to be burned to-morrer night, so there! Him and me's changed places. He's a Gummidge and I'm a Guy.'

Gummidge stretched out his stiff arm, snatched the hat out of John's hand and pulled it over his eyes again.

'But you don't want to be burned, do you?' asked Susan coaxingly.

'There you go again,' snapped Gummidge, 'there you go again worriting me with your daft questions. How do I know whether I wants to be burned or not till I *has* been burned. It'll be warm anyways. I'll have a lovely great bonfire all to myself and folks'll sing songs at me and set off fireworks at me.'

Gummidge smiled happily as he spoke of the fireworks, and the sight of his beaming face made Susan feel it would be dreadful to lose him.

'Where is the real Guy?' asked John.

Gummidge scowled so suddenly that two or three little trickles of dried mud ran down from the furrows in his forehead.

'I'm the real Guy,' he answered. 'I don't know where him that used to be Guy's gone, and I don't care. It were like this. I were going for a walk and I seed the

Guy sitting in a cowshed. He were wearing check
trousers and he had a blue shirt that had a bit took out
of it by a hot iron and he'd got a fine black coat with
dangling bits on it –'

'With dangling bits?' repeated Susan.

'I think he means a tail-coat,' John told her.

'Ooh aye!' agreed Gummidge, 'dangling bits it had
– same as the swallows wears. Well, as I was saying, him
and me changed clothes and then we had a bit of an
argufying because *I* wanted his necktie to go with my
collar and *he* wanted my collar to go with his necktie. I
said one of us ought to have both and I'd be the one.'

Gummidge paused to stretch one leg covered in ragged
black and white check out in front of him.

'What happened then?' asked Susan.

'The Guy said *he* ought to be the one and he said
it such a lot of times that I fell into a sulk. When I
come to the Guy had gone, so I says to myself I says,
"I'll be Guy and that'll learn him." And then Tommy
Higginsthwaite come along and set me in a go-cart.
I've never been one to be made a fuss of, but I'll be made
a fuss of to-morrer night.'

Gummidge stopped talking, jerked up his right arm,
and with his twiggy fingers pulled the big tweed hat over
his face.

Susan was just going to ask another question when she
heard Tommy Higginsthwaite's voice again. He was
singing, at least he was trying to sing –

> '*Guy, Guy, Guy,*
> *String him up on high.*
> *Put him on the chimney pot*
> *And there let him cry.*'

John looked at Susan and Susan looked at John.
They were both thinking the same thing – somehow
or other they must stop Worzel Gummidge from

being burned. They wished they had time to make some plan, but there wasn't any time because as soon as Tommy Higginsthwaite had grunted 'Good evening' to them, he seized the handles of the go-cart and began to push it down the road.

'We'll help you if you like,' said John.

'Of course we will,' added Susan.

Tommy Higginsthwaite jerked the go-cart so violently that Gummidge's head flopped and flopped.

'I'd sooner push it myself,' said Tommy, 'and I'd sooner get the pennies myself. It's my Guy, isn't it?'

'We don't want pennies –' began Susan, and John spoke furiously –

'She was only trying to help.'

'I don't want no help,' said Tommy.

'All right,' snapped Susan, 'I don't want to help you then. You're a very very horrid rude little boy!'

It was then that the dreadful thing happened. Susan was trying to think of an answer and so was John when suddenly a husky voice spoke –

'You'd best mind your manners, Tommy Higginsthwaite. Ooh aye! you'd best mind your manners.'

Tommy Higginsthwaite dropped the handles of the go-cart and let it slither forward. Then he said, 'You hold your tongue, Master John!'

'I didn't say a word,' said John.

Susan went to the front of the go-cart and looked pleadingly at Gummidge, whose hat was still pulled right over his eyes. She took hold of one of his twiggy fingers and stroked it.

'Do be quiet, Gummidge,' whispered Susan.

Worzel Gummidge was quiet, but John and Tommy Higginsthwaite went on quarrelling –

'I didn't say a word, I tell you.'

'Oh! you big story!'

Gummidge snatched his hand away from Susan's, raised his head and shouted, 'You'd best mind your manners, Tommy Higginsthwaite.'

'There you go again!' said Tommy.

'I tell you I didn't speak,' John sounded angry.

'You'll be telling me next that the Guy spoke.'

'P'raps he did,' said Susan.

Once more she clutched at Gummidge's hand. She felt a sort of quiver in the twiggy fingers, and remembered how once she had held the stem of a young pine-tree in the Spring and had felt how alive it was. But though she held tightly on to the fingers nothing could keep Gummidge quiet.

''Course it were me that spoke,' he said.

It really was rather a dreadful moment: Susan, understood, John understood, Worzel Gummidge understood everything. But Tommy Higginsthwaite didn't understand anything. He gave a loud sniff that was meant to be rude, and said, 'First you say you did speak and then you say you didn't. Anyone would think you were daft.'

Before John could think of an answer there were more words from the go-cart – 'It's you that's daft, Tommy Higginsthwaite, ooh aye, it's you that's daft.'

John gasped and Susan gasped. Only Worzel Gummidge, his hat pulled well down over his eyes, seemed to be calm and sulky.

Tommy Higginsthwaite snatched up the handles of the go-cart.

'You wait and see,' he said, 'you wait and see – that's all. I'm off. I'm not going to wait and be made a mock of by you.'

Before John or Susan could think of anything to say, Tommy Higginsthwaite had pushed the go-cart beyond the light of the hurricane lantern. They heard the clattery sound of his boots and the squeaking of the go-cart and the even worse squeak of his voice as he shouted, 'Penny for the Guy! Penny for the Guy!'

'I'm sick and tired of Gummidge,' said John. 'Now he's made another enemy for us.'

'I think he meant to help,' argued Susan. 'I really do think he meant to help. After all, Tommy *was* rude when I asked to push the go-cart. I only wanted to because I thought we might rescue Worzel Gummidge.'

'He's not worth rescuing,' snapped John, but all the same he hurried along beside Susan. They were both thinking the same thing and they were both hoping that Tommy Higginsthwaite would leave the go-cart outside another cottage.

The beech-leaves didn't help them much. They rustled and whispered underneath their shoes as they walked down the road. The lantern behaved badly too; sometimes it flared up, and at other times it left them nearly in the dark.

On and on went Tommy Higginsthwaite and on and on went his voice – 'Penny for the Guy! Penny for the Guy!' The figure in the go-cart was so quiet that John and Susan began to wonder if they had just dreamed the whole thing.

After a bit the go-cart stopped with a last squeak of its wheels. A gate squeaked too: there was a bumping sound and Tommy pushed the go-cart just inside his own garden.

The children waited until he had stumped up the path, until a door had been shut behind him and a red glow from a kitchen window had told them that Mrs Higginsthwaite had carried the lamp away from the door.

'Now!' said Susan.

'Now!' echoed John. He tiptoed into the cottage garden and wheeled the go-cart as quietly as possible into the road. Nobody spoke a word until Worzel Gummidge had been pushed round a bend in the winding village street.

'Good!' said Susan. 'Now, where shall we take him?'

'Back to the farm, I should think. We'll hide him in a loft or somewhere until after to-morrow.'

The go-cart gave a sudden jerk as Worzel Gummidge lurched sideways. Then he spoke indignantly –

'If you hide me I'll seek, and I'll find myself again as easy as mice finds cheese. Ooh aye! that I will.'

'But Gummidge, dear, we're only trying to rescue you.' Susan spoke pleadingly, but Worzel Gummidge sounded very cross.

'There's a deal too much rescuin' goin' on hereabouts. Cats rescues birds out of nests and stoats rescues rabbits out of hedges. Fisher-folks rescues fish out of streams. Interferin', that's what I calls it.'

'But we don't want you to be burned,' said John.

'There you go again talkin' selfish. It's not what you wants: it's what I wants. Dog-in-the-manger – that's what you are – trying to stop other folks from having a good warm-up.'

Gummidge's voice grew louder and presently he began to sing. His voice was rather like the creaking of a rusty gate.

'Please to remember the Fifth of November,' he sang. 'Penny for the Guy! Penny for the Guy.'

'Do be quiet,' said John. 'People will think it's us.'

'They always do,' agreed Susan, 'and we always get into trouble.'

Gummidge stopped in the middle of his song and raised his voice more loudly than ever.

'I wants my pennies and I'm going to shout for 'em. Penny for the Guy! Penny for the Guy! Penny for the Guy!'

John and Susan were not really surprised to hear the sharp click of a latch and the sharper click-click-clacketing of Mrs Bloomsbury-Barton's high heels as she hurried down the brick path of her garden.

It seemed as though they never could meet Gum-

midge without meeting Mrs Bloomsbury-Barton too:
it was a great pity.

John pulled Susan back into the shadows by the wall
and turned down the hurricane lamp. The two of them
held their breath as they watched the light of Mrs
Bloomsbury-Barton's electric torch bobbing nearer and
nearer to them.

'Penny for the Guy!' bawled Gummidge as she
stepped into the road. 'Penny for the poor old Guy.'

John and Susan blinked as the torch-light was turned
towards their faces.

'My dear children,' said Mrs Bloomsbury-Barton.
'Surely Mrs Braithewaite does not allow you to shout and
yell about the village like this.'

'Well, you see –' began Susan, and she blinked again,
'you see –'

It was then that the second dreadful thing happened.

'Guy! Guy! Guy! Feathers in yer eye. Won't you spare
a penny for the poor old Guy,' shouted Gummidge.

Now it so happened that some of the feathers from
Mrs Bloomsbury-Barton's ridiculous hat *were* very nearly
drooping into her eyes. John simply couldn't help giving
a little giggle when he noticed them. It was only quite a
tiny giggle but Mrs Bloomsbury-Barton heard.

'You are the most excessively impertinent little boy
I have ever met in my life. I shall certainly consider it
my duty to write to your mother, and I shall advise Mrs
Braithewaite not to let you go to the fireworks to-morrow
evening.'

'Oh! but please,' said Susan, 'please, you don't understand. John didn't speak at all. The – the – person who
spoke was –'

'Guy! Guy! Guy!' came the voice from the go-cart.

Mrs Bloomsbury-Barton turned so quickly on John
that her petticoats made a swishy sound.

'John,' she said, 'I am surprised and hurt.'

'Please,' gulped John. 'Please, I didn't say a word. It was –' Susan finished the sentence for him. She felt so cross with Gummidge that she didn't care if she was telling tales.

'It was this person in the go-cart,' she said.

Mrs Bloomsbury-Barton stopped looking at John or Susan and stared at Gummidge. His coat-sleeves, which were much too long for his arms, dangled over the sides of the go-cart. His hat was half over his face and he looked exactly like a very limp and badly-made Guy Fawkes.

Mrs Bloomsbury-Barton spoke in a really terrible voice.

'Are you trying to make me believe that this stuffed creature spoke?' she enquired.

Gummidge answered before John or Susan could think what to say.

'Believe what you likes,' he said. 'Believe what you likes, it don't make no difference to me. Stuffed yourself, and badly stuffed too!'

Before he had finished speaking Worzel Gummidge began to get out of the go-cart. Mrs Bloomsbury-Barton gave a little jump backwards on her high-heeled shoes and then dropped her torch so that only the flickering light from the hurricane lantern showed what Gummidge was doing. He moved more quickly than usual as he tugged at the coat tails which seemed to have got entangled in the wheels. Before John or Susan had made up their minds what to do, he had shambled away into the darkness.

Everybody gasped a little, but Mrs Bloomsbury-Barton gasped the loudest. Then she said, 'If that is your idea of a joke, John and Susan, it is a very poor and badly-mannered joke.'

Now until then, the children had not thought that Worzel Gummidge's queer behaviour was at all funny. In fact, they had felt almost as angry with him as Mrs

Bloomsbury-Barton was. But now as she stood there clicking her torch on and off and asking questions they found it very difficult not to laugh and could only answer her questions in a choky, jerky sort of way. You see she asked such queer questions considering that she was asking them about a scarecrow – Where did Gummidge live and did he come from a *nice* home and who were his parents and how old was he?

At last, after they had muttered, 'We don't know' about half a dozen times Mrs Bloomsbury-Barton let them go.

'All most unsatisfactory,' she said, 'and it is evident that you have made a most unsuitable friend. I shall speak to Mrs Braithewaite. Now you had better go back to the farm.'

John and Susan went gladly, but not to the farm. Instead they pushed the go-cart in the direction that Gummidge had taken, and then went along the little path that led to the Play-close where the huge bonfire was stacked all ready for the next day's celebrations.

On their way they passed the little village shop, but for once they did not stop to flatten their noses against the glass that separated them from the jars of sweets and the collection of marbles and whips and tops. They did not even remember that they had meant to buy fireworks.

CHAPTER XII

FIREWORKS AND MATCHES

—

JUST as they reached the Play-close some clouds which had been hiding the moon were kind enough to move away so that the children were able to see the huge bonfire. As they came closer they saw a familiar figure lolling against a big log on the top of it, and they heard the sheep-like cough that was so different from every other sound in the world.

John left the go-cart and they both ran forward. It wasn't until they had nearly reached the foot of the bonfire that Susan suddenly remembered.

'Oh! dear,' she gasped, '*that* can't be Gummidge because *he* was wearing check trousers. That must be the Guy who changed clothes with him. I do wish he hadn't got his back turned.'

'But we heard Gummidge cough,' argued John.

'P'raps Guys cough like Gummidges.' Susan tried to sound hopeful but she didn't feel it. And then they heard the cough again, and both ran round to the other side of the bonfire.

There, looking very unhappy in the moonlight, stood Worzel Gummidge. At his feet was a collection of fireworks, a packet of matches, some little bits of stick and odds and ends of litter. He was talking to himself in a distracted sort of way.

'It's too bad. It's a great deal too bad. Ooh aye! So it is and I'd be crying like a thunder-shower if it wasn't such a fine night.'

'Why do you want to cry?' asked John; and Susan said, 'I didn't know you could cry.'

'No more I can't,' complained Gummidge, 'no more I can't – not without it's raining. If it were raining to-night, I'd have my hat off and the drops would be rolling down my cheeks and getting caught up in my shirt. The weather's a deal sight too contrary. I might be feeling as cheerful and reckless as anything on a wet night when all the tears gets wasted.'

Gummidge stooped down and picked up a box of matches. The tails of his shabby coat made him look like some giant rook.

'I can cry in any sort of weather,' boasted Susan.

'Maybe, but then you're made so queer. I never knew but one scarecrow who would cry after the rain stopped. Her face was stuffed with sponge, poor thing, so you'd got to squeeze it or hit it, but that were easy.'

'It sounds rather unkind though,' said Susan. 'I should think almost everyone would cry if you squeezed their faces.'

'Not me, I don't.' Gummidge sounded so miserable that Susan gave him a little pat. 'Not me, I don't. Anyone would want to cry if their trousy pockets were full of interesting things, and the trousies were being wore by someone else and he were sulking in 'em. When I changed clothes with that Guy I didn't know his pockets was empty. 'Tain't fair.'

Gummidge sat down with a jerk and looked so sulky that John asked a question.

'What have you got in your pockets?'

'It's not what I've got in my pockets,' said Gummidge, and he scratched his chin with a squib. 'It's what *he's* got in my pockets. There's a grasshopper that got tired of hopping last August and there's a bit of putty and there's Earthy's banana skin what was her favourite handkercher and there's – there's –'

Here Gummidge gave a sort of choking sob and then another one.

'What else?' asked Susan soothingly.

'My – my rabbit,' gulped Gummidge – 'gettin' so tame it were, *and* earnin' its own living by cuttin' my hair.'

'But rabbits don't cut hair,' John objected.

'Mine did.'

'Would it cut ours?' asked Susan.

Gummidge looked at her in a pitying way. 'Not likely,' he answered. 'My hair's better nor what yours is. Your hair is just like frayed out string – no nourishment in it. Mine's different.'

'I should think it is. Yours –'

'Mine's all green and sprouty and tasty. The rabbit crops it as close as anything. Now it'll grow long again, and it'll push my hat off my head. My hairbrush has gone to sleep for the winter. I've never been so glad as when that rabbit mistook my pocket for a burrow. I were lying down at the time. Like this.' Gummidge jerked himself backwards and lay quite still. Presently he shut one eye, and John, fearing he had fallen into another sulk, asked a question about more cheerful things.

'Where did you get the fireworks?'

'Bought 'em,' answered Gummidge. 'Bought 'em with the money in that tin that Tommy Higginsthwaite was carrying round.'

He opened his eye just as Susan was going to open her mouth and went on hastily. 'They were my pennies, weren't they? I were the Guy, weren't I, else why did Tommy Higginsthwaite keep on shouting, "Penny for the Guy"?'

Susan felt rather doubtful about this, but because she didn't want Gummidge to sulk again she said, 'You've got lots of fireworks. There must have been an awful lot of pennies in the tin.'

'May have been,' said Gummidge, 'or may not. I couldn't get at 'em. There weren't nobody in the shop when I went in just now so I took what I liked and left the tin. I'd sooner have my rabbit though. And there were other things in my pockets. There were half a rake with only two teeth missing what I'd been saving up for Earthy. She might be wanting artificial teeth but she'll never have 'em now – not if the Guy won't come down.'

Gummidge sat up, tugged at a branch that was sticking out from the bottom of the bonfire, and shook it until the flag on the top rocked.

'Now then,' he said, 'just you listen to him when I shouts at him.'

Neither Susan nor John had ever heard a scarecrow shouting before. The sound reminded them of the mooing of a cow, the coughing of a sheep and the swinging of a gate on rusty hinges. They felt quite glad when Gummidge stopped shouting and said 'Now then just listen.'

A long silence followed his words. The Guy on the top of the bonfire was still swaying a little, but as his hat (or rather Gummidge's old hat) was tilted over his face they could not tell if he minded.

'He doesn't say anything,' said Susan.

'That's what I asked you to listen at,' replied Gummidge sulkily. 'I'm tired of argufying and I'm tired of asking. I'm just going to begin the fireworks. Gimme the matches.'

'I'm sure,' began Susan, 'I'm quite sure you aren't allowed to play with matches.'

'I feel that reckless I'd play with the sun if I could get near enough.'

His words made the children feel reckless too. John picked up a Catherine Wheel, Susan took a handful of squibs, Gummidge looked moodily at a Roman Candle and then they all began to strike matches.

Now matches by themselves don't make much of a display, and nothing happened at all when they tried to let off the fireworks.

'Mine's damp,' said John at last.

'Mine are all sopping,' said Susan.

''Course they are,' agreed Gummidge. 'I dipped most of 'em in a bucket that were standing outside of the shop.'

'What a mad thing to do,' said John.

''Tweren't mad – 'twere sensible. You damp a fire down when you want it to keep in.'

'Oh dear!' said Susan, because she really was disap-

pointed about the fireworks. 'Don't you know that a fire
is quite, quite different?'

Gummidge looked at her in a sad pitying sort of way
and then spoke very slowly.

'It's different in one way and it's the same in another.
A fire doesn't go bouncing up into the air or whizzing
itself at you, but if you wants it to last longer you damps
it down. Trouble with you is you've not been eddicated.'

Gummidge looked so fiercely at the children that John
snapped at him, 'We do know that fireworks shouldn't
be damped.'

'Ever tried?' asked Gummidge.

They felt too annoyed to answer, so he went on. 'You
don't know what you're talking about.'

'We aren't talking,' said Susan.

'Then you don't know what you're thinking about.
Fireworks is terrible hasty impatient sort of things, and
these ones has got to learn to keep in. Why they won't
go out till Midsummer.'

Susan stamped her foot and Gummidge looked down
at it while she replied: 'Of course they can't go out if
they won't even light.'

'That's what I were saying,' said Gummidge and he
smiled happily.

John looked at Susan and Susan looked at John.
They knew Gummidge was wrong, but he was a frightfully difficult person to argue with.

'If – ' began Susan.

'But –' began John.

Then they stopped again and looked up at the moon
while they tried to think of something really clever to
say. They could hear Gummidge creaking as he moved
about. Then they heard him cough but they felt too
cross to answer him. Presently they heard another
sound, a sort of fizzing and crackling. They looked down

and saw that the scarecrow had set the whole packet of matches on fire. Before they could do anything about it he had kicked the blazing bundle on to the bonfire.

'Oh! look what you've done!' cried Susan as a pile of dried bracken caught fire. 'Now the Guy will be burned.'

'That's what he thinks,' said Gummidge, 'but he thinks wrong. He's not going to be burned – not in my clothes and my rabbit in his pocket.'

'Gummidge, come back,' said Susan as the scarecrow shambled past her. 'John! Stop him, he's climbing right up the bonfire.'

But Worzel Gummidge took no notice at all. He went scrambling up one side of the bonfire, tugging at twigs and branches and shuffling about on paper. Luckily the fire had only just begun to flare dangerously when he seized the Guy's leg and tugged. In a moment the pair of them had rolled down the side of the bonfire and were safely on the grass. The children saw a very small rabbit dart out of the Guy's pocket, and scurry away to the hedge.

Gummidge sat up and changed hats with the Guy. At least he snatched his own one from the Guy's head and slammed down the one he had been wearing in a way that would certainly have hurt anyone whose head had not been made from a yellow croquet ball.

'Lend us a hand, can't you?' said Gummidge impatiently.

'Lend you a hand with what?' asked John.

'With the Guy o' course. I'm going to put him in the go-cart and take him up to Ten-acre so's he can do some rook-scaring. He said he'd change places and so he shall.'

'Don't make such a noise,' begged Susan.

'It's my own noise, isn't it?'

'But people are coming. I can see lanterns,' whispered Susan.

It was quite true. There was a sound of voices, and

bobbing lights began to appear on the edge of the Play-close. The lanterns came nearer and nearer as Gum-midge, Susan, and John half-lifted and half-dragged the Guy into one of the damp ditches that bounded the Play-close. He did not speak or struggle, and it was difficult to believe he had ever spoken in his life. A few chips on the yellow croquet ball marked his eyes and ears. There was a big slit for a mouth and a blob of paint for a nose. He had mallets for legs and his arms looked very wirey.

'Maybe he'll sulk for a year,' said Gummidge. 'Terrible obstinate creature he is. Ooh aye!'

'Hush!' whispered Susan.

'I'll hush when I wants to,' said Gummidge.

Then, before Susan or John could do anything to stop him, he had gripped a tuft of grass and dragged himself out of the ditch. In the flickering light of the bonfire the children could see him shuffling across the Play-close. When he reached the go-cart, he sat down in it with a jerk which set it moving for a few yards. Mean-while three bobbing lanterns came nearer and nearer.

'I think,' whispered Susan, 'I *think* that's Mrs Blooms-bury-Barton and – and – yes, it *is* Tommy Higgins-thwaite and there's Mrs Higginsthwaite too.'

'Don't let them hear us,' whispered John.

But Mrs Bloomsbury-Barton and Mrs Higginsthwaite and Tommy were all talking much too loudly and exci-tedly to hear anything, even each other. Anyway, nobody stopped much to listen to what anyone else was saying.

Mrs Higginsthwaite was shouting that it was a shame, so it was, for anybody to light the bonfire on the day before Guy Fawkes Day and that if she caught them she didn't know what she wouldn't do to them.

Mrs Bloomsbury-Barton said she was quite sure she had seen somebody moving about. By the time she had repeated this three times, while Mrs Higginsthwaite managed to remark four times that she didn't know what the world was coming to, Tommy Higginsthwaite had found the go-cart. He pushed it forward so that the light from the fire flickered on Gummidge's obstinate face and queer clothes and stiff limbs.

'Let's burn the Guy, Mum,' shouted Tommy. 'Let's burn the Guy. It's a shame to waste the bonfire.'

Susan and John clutched each other. They forgot to notice that brambles were sticking hooks into their legs and that nettles were stinging them on the bare places above socks and stockings. They forgot everything except that Worzel Gummidge seemed to be in terrible danger again.

For the first time they were quite pleased to hear Mrs Bloomsbury-Barton's voice.

'Bring your lantern nearer, Tommy. A little closer, please. That's right, dear. Yes, I thought I was not mistaken.'

Mrs Bloomsbury-Barton peered so closely into Gummidge's face that Susan felt more unhappy than ever. She was sure that his enemy's angry expression would send Gummidge into one of his very longest sulks.

Then, while Tommy was still begging to be allowed to burn the Guy, another light came bobbing across the Play-close.

'Land sake!' exclaimed Mrs Higginsthwaite. 'It's the policeman.'

It was the policeman. He came very quietly across the grass and now stood flashing his torch from the sulky face of Gummidge in the go-cart to the puzzled face of Tommy and Mrs Higginsthwaite. John and Susan held their breath and peeped through the grass that fringed the top of the ditch.

'Good evening, constable,' said Mrs Bloomsbury-Barton in the sort of voice that she generally kept for tea-party use. 'Will you please do your duty at once, and arrest this man. He has stolen Mrs Higginsthwaite's go-cart and her son's money-box. Earlier this evening he was extremely impertinent to me. And now, I suppose he has lit this bonfire.'

The policeman straightened his helmet, tugged at his tunic and looked important as he asked, 'And what man would that be, ma'am?'

Mrs Bloomsbury-Barton pointed to Gummidge.

Once more the policeman shone his torch on to the scarecrow's turnipy face.

'There's some mistake,' he said slowly. 'That's only the old Guy Fawkes that was being wheeled round the village.'

'I tell you,' Mrs Bloomsbury-Barton's voice was quite squeaky with temper. 'I tell you he is only pretending to be a Guy Fawkes.'

'Then he's a rare good pretender, ma'am,' said the policeman.

'An excellent actor,' agreed Mrs Bloomsbury-Barton. 'I will admit that. But I can assure you that when he was being pushed round the village this evening, he insulted me. Naturally, not believing that a Guy Fawkes could speak, I reproved the two children who were in charge of him. And then – this – creature got up and walked away *with* the money-box.'

The policeman gave Gummidge a shake, and then he shook his own head slowly from side to side.

'Seeing's believing,' he said. 'I don't know what you saw, ma'am, but this here that I'm seeing is a Guy Fawkes.'

'I – I shall send for the Inspector,' almost shrieked Mrs Bloomsbury-Barton.

'Just as you like, ma'am,' said the policeman. 'Then you won't be wanting me any more.'

He turned off his torch and was just going to move away when Tommy Higginsthwaite spoke.

'Come to think of it –' he said.

Mrs Bloomsbury-Barton patted him on the back. 'Yes, Tommy,' she said between pats. 'Speak up bravely and tell the constable all you know.'

And then, while John and Susan let insects crawl down their necks and brambles drag at their legs, Tommy Higginsthwaite told the story of the quarrel he had had with them.

'Come to think of it –' he said, 'the voice didn't sound like Master John's. It was deeper and louder – more like a man's.'

'Sneak,' muttered John. 'Sneak to give Gummidge away!' But Susan pinched him because Mrs Bloomsbury-Barton was speaking again. She sounded so certain about Gummidge being a man that the policeman turned back and once more shone his torch full in the scarecrow's face. Then he shook him by the arm. There was no answer, only a rustle of straw and the squeaking of the go-cart's wheels.

'I've done a lot of queer things in the course of my duty but I've never been asked to arrest a Guy Fawkes *yet*,' said the policeman, 'no, nor not a wax doll either.'

'But I tell you,' Mrs Bloomsbury-Barton's voice was even more fretful than usual, 'I tell you I recognize the man's clothes, his absurd tail-coat, his hat and his muffler.'

The policeman didn't answer but he lifted Gummidge's hat from his turnipy head. His torch lit up the close-cropped green sprouts and the sulky mouth and the knobbly nose.

'And what would we do with *that* at the police station?' asked the policeman.

'That is for you to say,' replied Mrs Bloomsbury-Barton in her haughtiest voice. 'I beg you to take him away at once.'

'All right! All right!' said the policeman. 'But we'll soon see which of us is right, madam.'

He clicked out his torch and began to wheel the go-cart across the Play-close. Mrs Bloomsbury-Barton and the Higginsthwaites followed him.

'Oh dear,' sighed Susan, 'Poor, poor Gummidge!'

John repeated the policeman's question. 'I should like to know what they'll do with him at the police station?'

Susan did not answer because she was feeling so unhappy. The Guy Fawkes did not answer either, but the rabbit hopped on to her lap and quivered its whiskers in a sympathetic and comforting way.

'Poor little thing,' said Susan. 'We'd better take it back to the farm with us. It can sleep with me.'

'No, with me,' said John as he stroked the rabbit's ears.

CHAPTER XIII

CONSTABLE GUMMIDGE

—

THE next morning, before she was quite wide awake, Susan had the feeling that something rather unhappy had happened. She opened one eye and was quite surprised to see that it was a bright morning, even though it was November. So it wasn't the weather that was wrong. Nor was there anything the matter with Mrs Braithewaite's temper either. Susan could hear her singing as she washed the hall floor. When Mrs Braithewaite was cross she banged and bumped, her bucket rattled and her broom thumped against the wainscoting. And there wasn't anything wrong in the farmyard either or Farmer Braithewaite would not have been whistling so cheerfully.

Suddenly Susan remembered that Worzel Gummidge had been taken to the police station the night before. The thought jerked her wide awake and sent her out of bed in a hurry and tip-toeing into John's room without bothering to put on her slippers.

John was asleep, but Gummidge's rabbit was wide awake on the pillow. It flattened back its ears as Susan came in and then went on washing its face.

'John!' said Susan, 'Wake up!'

John grunted and snuggled his head more deeply down into the pillow. The rabbit stopped washing its face, and pushed its soft quivering nose towards him so that its whiskers tickled his eyelid; and then he really did wake up.

Susan sat on the edge of the bed and they talked and talked and talked about the dreadful problem of how to rescue Worzel Gummidge.

But the more they talked, the more difficult it all seemed.

'We might be able to get him out of an ordinary house,' said Susan, 'but not from a police station. And I don't see how we can even ask about him. It isn't as if –'

But before she could finish speaking the rabbit, who had been sitting on John's pillow all the time, suddenly decided to go exploring.

It hopped down from the bed and then, with an impertinent little jerk of its white scut, went out into the passage.

John and Susan followed in their pyjamas because there was no time to think of dressing-gowns.

Down the stairs flopped the rabbit, pausing every now and then to flatten itself against the skirting board. But every time John or Susan reached the step above down it went – flop – flop – flop until it reached the hall.

'Sakes alive!' said Mrs Braithewaite as the rabbit ran between her feet on its way to the front door, and nearly tripped her up. 'These cats will be the death of me.'

Then she looked up and saw the children.

'And you'll be the death of yourselves,' she said, 'running about in your bare feet.'

'It's the rabbit,' said John, and diving in front of Mrs Braithewaite he snatched the rabbit by the ears just before the door opened and the farmer came tramping into the hall.

They all talked about the rabbit at breakfast time. Mrs Braithewaite said she couldn't have any more animals in the house because she had enough bother with the cats and the sheep-dog, the lambs at one time of year, the chickens at another, and kittens all the season through.

Farmer Braithewaite suggested 'pie' to the rabbit even though it wobbled its nose at him. Then he laughed because Susan nearly cried and he said he hadn't meant it and that if she thought it was such an important rabbit she had better take it to the police station and make enquiries about its owner.

'It's tame, I can see that,' he said; 'and probably some child is crying its eyes out. Where did you find it?'

'On the Play-close last night,' said John. 'It *is* tame, isn't it?'

'And it *is* sweet, isn't it?' said Susan.

The rabbit was busy with a cabbage leaf, which had been given to it by Mrs Braithewaite. She was kind really, but she always pretended to be fierce.

'The best thing you can do,' she said, 'far the best thing is to take this rabbit round to all the cottages and try to find out who it belongs to.'

'Or we might take it to the police station,' said John. 'Policemen are supposed to find people that have lost things.'

'The other way on. The police find things that people have lost,' said Farmer Braithewaite. 'If you ask me though, policemen don't want to be bothered with rabbits.'

After breakfast, John buttoned the rabbit inside his overcoat and they went into the village.

The police station in Scatterbrook was only a little red cottage with a small garden in front and a bigger garden at the side. It looked friendlier in the summer time when the red flagged path, leading to the house, was bordered with marigolds and pansies, sweet williams and pinks. Now these had given way to a few blackened dahlias and the garden had rather a stern look.

John was holding the rabbit so Susan knocked at the door and, when it was opened by a tall man in shirt sleeves, she asked shyly, 'Please, can we see the Policeman?'

'You *are* seeing the policeman,' he said. Susan then saw that he was the policeman, only he looked so different in brown trousers and a pink and white shirt and no helmet, that she walked backwards down the steps.

'We're sorry,' said John politely, 'we didn't know you were having a holiday. We only came to ask if you could keep this rabbit for us until we can find the person it belongs to. Mrs Braithewaite won't let us have it at the farm.'

'It's a very nice rabbit,' added Susan, 'and quite tame.'

'I should think keeping rabbits is just about all he's good for,' said a voice.

There, standing behind the policeman, was the small bustling woman who was his wife.

'If he can't even keep his own uniform, I don't know what he can keep. He loses everything. I never knew such a man.'

The policeman looked, except for his size, very like a small boy who was being scolded, he rumpled his hair and said –

'If you'd been carrying a Guy Fawkes about you'd have wanted to brush your clothes. I should like to catch whoever made that Guy. It was stuffed with straw and covered with mud. After I'd brushed my uniform I hung it out on the line so as to get rid of the smell of turnip.'

Susan jumped from one foot to the other because she did so want to know what had happened to Worzel Gummidge, but she didn't dare to ask. John was not so frightened.

'Where is the Guy Fawkes?' he asked.

'The person who stole my uniform seems to have taken a fancy to the Guy Fawkes too,' said the policeman. 'I'd left it propped up against the outhouse door and when I went out at eleven o'clock to fetch in my uniform the Guy Fawkes had gone too. Wait till I catch the man who's stolen them – that's all . . .'

'Waiting won't catch anybody,' put in the policeman's wife. 'What you ought to do is to get on to your bicycle and go and find the man – that's what you ought to do.'

'But *please*, what about the rabbit?' asked Susan, feeling that something must be done to prevent the policeman from finding Gummidge again.

But the policeman seemed suddenly to have forgotten all about the rabbit. He had been looking down at his wife, and now he turned and followed her into the house, leaving John and Susan standing on the path. They waited for about half a minute, and then walked down between the dahlias to the little garden gate.

'It sounds awfully as though Gummidge must have taken the policeman's uniform,' said Susan.

'Of course he has; it's the sort of thing he would do. I wish Earthy would manage him better.'

Just then the rabbit wriggled its way out of John's hands, took a lolloping hop, then another one, and began to scurry down the road. The children followed it, but they didn't enjoy the chase so much as the rabbit did. On and on it went, flaunting its white scut in a most provoking way. Sometimes it even stopped to wash its face, but each time they nearly grabbed it, on it went, flicking and lolloping along the road.

It led them through a hedge and across a field, down a lane, into another lane and then it sat up and twitched its nose at them. 'You've led us a dance,' panted Susan, as she picked it up.

'You've led us a lollop,' gasped John. 'And now where are we?'

The sound of a motor-horn answered the question, and they went down the lane which widened and widened until it met the main road.

Someone in a blue helmet was standing with his back to them. His arms were stuck out sideways: two limp white gloves dangled from the end of his tunic cuffs.

'Gummidge,' whispered Susan, 'it must be Worzel Gummidge!'

Of course, it was Worzel Gummidge, wearing trousers so much too big for him that they looked like plus-fours. A little fringe of hay edged the tops of his huge boots and a tuft of hay peeped out from underneath his helmet.

'We must go and get him away from there,' said John.

'Not just now,' said Susan. 'Look, somebody's coming down the opposite lane. Let's hide behind the hedge and wait.'

So they slipped through an open gateway and crouched down in the angle of the hedge. Nearer and nearer to Gummidge came a small neat elderly man who was followed by a Labrador dog. When he reached the junction of the roads, he looked to the left and right to make sure that no traffic was coming either way. Then he walked to where Gummidge was standing, took a pair of spectacles out of his pocket, and asked, 'Which of these roads will take me to Scatterbrook?'

It may have been an accident or it may not, but as soon as the question was asked Worzel Gummidge dropped one of his arms so quickly that he sent the glasses flying out of the stranger's hand and on to the muddy road. There was a tinkle which told that at least one lens was broken.

'Now I shan't be able to read a word,' said the little man, as he picked up the glasses. 'Great nuisance being so short-sighted.' He took out his handkerchief and began to polish the spectacles.

'And now, can you tell me which of these roads will take me to Scatterbrook?'

Susan clutched John's arm as she waited for the answer.

'None of 'em will – nor any other road neither.'

'But I am staying in Penfold, and was told it was only a short walk from there to Scatterbrook.'

'Ooh aye!' agreed Gummidge. 'So 'tis.'

'Then which road shall I take?' The little man's voice sounded quite impatient.

'You'll not take any road, not if I can help it. That's what I'm here for to stop people takin' roads or anything else either.'

'I *beg* your pardon –' the little man put up one hand to his ear. He sounded unbelieving and yet rather annoyed too.

'And beggin's not allowed neither.'

Perhaps in a way it was lucky (though neither John nor Susan thought so at the moment) that the Labrador dog came sniffing across the road, and through a gap in the hedge.

Away went the rabbit from Susan's lap, away went the Labrador after it. There was a squeal from the rabbit, a scream from Susan, a shout from John, and then all four of them (except the poor little rabbit which was being carried) broke through the fence and across the road to where Worzel Gummidge and the stranger were standing.

The Labrador got there first, sat down and looked up at its master.

'Please, *please*,' cried Susan. 'Don't let him hurt it.'

'It's a tame rabbit,' added John.

'Hurt it!' said the little man. 'My dog has a mouth like velvet.' He stooped down and took the rabbit from the Labrador's gentle mouth. Then he handed it to Susan who saw that it was quite unhurt though its fur was rather damp and its eyes looked bigger than ever.

'I am sorry to have frightened you, my child,' he said, and he stroked the rabbit's velvety nose. 'It was bad of my dog to make a mistake like that. Is it your rabbit?'

'Poacher!' interrupted Gummidge furiously. 'Poacher! First you tries to steal roads, then you comes begging, and then you goes poaching!'

The little man went quite crimson in the face with surprise and anger as he put on his muddy-rimmed spectacles and peered through the broken smeary glass at Worzel Gummidge who had now snatched the rabbit from Susan and was trying to fit it into the breast-pocket of his tunic.

'I shall take your number, my man,' said the stranger, 'and I shall report your rudeness to the Chief Constable, who is a friend of mine.'

'You'll not take my number, nor my rabbit neither.'

Worzel Gummidge took two or three crab-like steps, and sat down on a heap of stones by the side of the road.

Suddenly Susan burst into tears – it was a thing she had not done for a very long time, but now she was upset over the affair of the dog and the rabbit and even

more worried over the strange behaviour of Gummidge.
He was such a confusing and muddling person.

'Dear me! dear me!' said the little man with the
muddied spectacles. 'Bless my soul! Don't cry like that,
my child. Nobody is angry with you.'

He took out a large clean handkerchief, smelling
faintly of tobacco and shaving-soap, and dabbed Susan's
face with it.

'Nobody is angry with *you*.'

The Labrador stood up on its hind-legs and with
a warm red tongue began to lick Susan's tears
away.

'Look, he's saying he is very sorry that he frightened
your rabbit.'

The Labrador finished saying 'sorry' with his tongue
and now began to say it with his huge black paws, and
said it so very strongly that he knocked Susan backwards
into the mud.

By the time she had been picked up and brushed
down, had her face washed by the Labrador, her hat
shaken by John, and her hands scrubbed with the
stranger's handkerchief, Worzel Gummidge had disappeared. Everybody had been too busy to notice him,
and only a few wisps of hay remained to show that he
had ever been near the stone-heap.

'Very abrupt sort of fellow that,' exclaimed the little
man. 'And now perhaps you can show me the way to
Scatterbrook.'

So because they were going his way they had no
chance to look for Gummidge.

It grew misty in the afternoon and by tea-time the
mist had turned to fog – a thick soft-looking fog that
reminded them of the cobwebs up in the loft. It cleared
a little in the evening but there was no moon and by
the time they reached the Play-close the few squibs

that were being let off gleamed queerly as though they were shining through a curtain.

John and Susan wandered about looking for Worzel Gummidge, because he had a way of turning up suddenly whenever there was any excitement. They thought that if he happened to be hiding in any chicken-run or ditch or out-house, the dim lights from the Playclose might attract him just as candles attract moths. They noticed that another bonfire had been built, but it was not so big as the last one.

'If we could only hear him cough,' said Susan.

But they heard nothing except the hissing and spitting, crackling, screaming, and banging of the fireworks. After a time they hurried back to the little shop in the village to buy fireworks of their own. By the time they came back the red-golden light of the bonfire was shredding the fog and a lot of people were running towards it. John and Susan followed them.

Just in front of them was the policeman's wife, and as she ran she screamed. 'Save him! Murder! Fire! My poor husband's fallen into a faint on the top of the bonfire! Whatever shall I do? Whatever shall I do?'

John and Susan scurried past her and were just in time to see a figure in a blue helmet lolling on the top of the bonfire.

'Gummidge!' said Susan. 'Oh dear!'

'My husband!' said the policeman's wife.

'He'll be burned,' said John.

But nobody was burned because the real village policeman pushed his way through the crowd, jerked at a branch on the top of the bonfire and pulled it away.

There was a crashing sound, something came tumbling down and lay beside the bonfire.

'So that's where my uniform got to,' said the policeman as he stooped to pick up his battered helmet from where it lay beside the croquet-ball head of the Guy Fawkes. He tugged at the Guy's wiry arms and dragged it away while its croquet-mallet legs made dark streaks in the wet grass.

'Well, of all mysterious things!' exclaimed the policeman's wife.

But John and Susan knew there was nothing so very mysterious about it at all, because they understood that once more Worzel Gummidge had changed clothes with the Guy Fawkes.

'I hope he kept the rabbit,' said Susan.

'I hope he's found all the things in his pockets,' said John.

CHAPTER XIV
THE KINDNESS OF GUMMIDGE
—

Snow had been falling all night, and, except for the blue sky, there was scarcely a scrap of colour to be seen anywhere. The trees and hedges looked as though they had been dipped in silver, and whenever John or Susan brushed against a twig they heard the very very faintest tinkly sounds because it was still freezing.

The snow under their feet squeaked as they walked and the sides of the lane that led up towards Ten-acre Field showed the tiny footprints of birds.

It was a long time since they had seen anything of Worzel Gummidge or Earthy, his wife, so they had gone for a walk to look for them.

'If he's anywhere about we ought to be able to see him to-day,' said Susan. 'He's certain to show up well against the snow.'

'Yes,' agreed John, 'but if he happened to be sulking

when the snow first began to fall I don't suppose he'd bother to move. He may be buried.'

The children thought about this rather gloomily until they came to a very dishevelled haystack – the one where Worzel Gummidge had changed boots with the sleeping tramp. The stack had been tidy enough then, but now it looked like the nest of some giant sparrow. A pair of bottle-straws lay just outside a sort of tunnel that seemed to lead to the middle of the stack. As soon as she saw them Susan said, 'I'm sure those are Gummidge's boots. Nobody else would tie tarred string on to bottle-straws.'

'And there's Earthy's apron,' said John. 'I'm going to go inside the haystack.'

John lay flat on his front and began to wriggle his way through the straw tunnel while Susan watched him rather anxiously. Gummidge had a great many queer friends and she was afraid that John might meet one of the fiercer sort of scarecrows. But as it would have been silly to argue with a pair of heels, which was all that showed of her brother, Susan began to look about her.

Certainly the outside of the stack was very untidy. Armfuls of hay lay scattered all over the place. There were two or three carrots, an empty sardine tin, a rusty frying-pan and some pieces of sacking. There were also a number of very curious-looking marks in the snow – boot-marks and stumpy sort of marks and the tiny paw-marks of an animal.

Susan was puzzling over these when John joined her, and said that there was nothing but a big hollow in the middle of the haystack. His hair stood on end and every now and then he sneezed because the inside of the stack had been so dusty.

'Look!' said Susan, and she pointed to the trail of queer marks that led right across the field to the far hedge. 'I think some scarecrows have gone for a walk.'

'And those paw-marks must belong to Gummidge's rabbit,' said John. 'Come along!'

When they were half way across the field John suddenly stopped, went down on his knees and scooped up a little handful of sawdust.

'Oh!' said Susan. 'That must mean that Hannah Harrow is with them. Don't you remember the mice always get at her and her sawdust stuffing always leaks out. Poor Hannah Harrow!'

The sawdust trail grew thicker and thicker, so thick that the children began to feel really anxious about Hannah Harrow's health. She was not a particularly interesting scarecrow and rather a dismal one, but she had always been kind to them.

'I wonder,' said Susan, as they reached the hedge, 'I wonder who we'll see on the other side. I'm almost afraid to look.'

But, when at last they rested their chins on the snow-covered hedge and stood on tip-toe to peep over it, they could see nothing at all. Beyond was another sloping field, but there was not a mark on it except the little splayed claw-prints of birds.

It was all very mysterious.

'Gummidge!' called John. 'Gummidge! Worzel Gummidge.'

There was silence for a moment or two and then a voice answered –

'Mr Gummidge isn't here. It's only us.'

'Who are you?' asked Susan.

'It's Mrs Gummidge, Mrs Earthy Mangold Gummidge. I've got Hannah down here in the ditch and how I'm to get her home I don't know.'

Earthy's voice sounded so sad that John and Susan fought their way through the hedge, though the shaken snow gave them cold neck-baths and the twigs scratched them. When they got to the other side they saw a strange sight.

Sitting upright in a deep ditch at the foot of the hedge was Hannah Harrow. She was wearing a small round fruit basket instead of a hat, and the tarred string that she called her hair was arranged in an untidy bun over her right ear. Round her neck was Gummidge's rabbit. Every time it twitched its nose, it tickled Hannah under the chin. Beside them sat Earthy Mangold, her nice little brown potatoish face very sad.

'She's got the mice again,' said Earthy. 'She's got em' worse than she's ever had 'em. It's all along of sleeping in the haystack last night – fair riddled with mice it is.'

'They stuffed me with sawdust – that's the trouble,' said Hannah in a faint voice.

Earthy turned towards her quite indignantly.

'That's not all the trouble – not by a long way. I warned you what would happen if you ate cheese for supper. Time and again I've said you'll never get rid of the mice if you will keep on eating what *they* fancies.'

'I know,' agreed Hannah meekly, 'but the trouble is to find out what they don't fancy.'

She looked so sad and Earthy so annoyed that Susan thought she had better change the subject, so she asked where Gummidge was.

'You'd better ask Hannah that,' snapped Earthy.

The limp scarecrow raised her head and the children noticed that sawdust tears were trickling down her cheeks.

'It's all because of me that he's where he is and I'd bob my lovely hair if I could find him.'

'But where is he?' asked Susan.

Hannah's reply was rather confusing.

'We was just beginning to look when I was took bad. Came over all queer, I did, and begun to sag. I've suffered from sagging ever since I were first stuffed –

mice and sagging. One thing leads to another as you might say. Have you ever suffered from sagging, Miss?'

'No,' replied Susan. 'Where *is* Gummidge?'

Hannah sobbed for a few moments before answering. 'It's all my fault he's wherever he is. Sooner than let this have happened I'd have cut off my left hand, and that's the best one, seeing as how it has ever so many more fingers than what the other has.'

'Oh dear!' sighed Susan. 'She isn't very clever, is she? Earthy, don't *you* know where Worzel Gummidge is?'

Earthy sat up with an indignant jerk which made Hannah, who was leaning against her, sag more than ever.

'He went out ever so early this morning to get some cheese for Hannah's mice. He thought if as how he were to put more cheese *outside* of her than what she's got *inside* of her, the mice would come out, and she'd feel a bit easier. And so –'

'What a good idea,' interrupted John.

'Yes,' Earthy's voice sounded very proud. 'Worzel always was one for ideas.'

'And did he get the cheese?' asked Susan.

Earthy's little brown face puckered so sadly that the children were afraid she was going to cry. She stopped to rearrange the rabbit round Hannah's neck before she answered, and Susan noticed that she dabbed at her eyes with its ears.

'I don't know what he's done nor yet where he is,' said Earthy sadly. 'Lost in the snow maybe. We was just starting out to look for him when Hannah started sagging. I've wrapped her up warm with the rabbit round her neck and now there's nothing for it but to go back home and fetch some more stuffing.'

'Can't we help?' asked John.

'We'd love to help,' added Susan. Then she scrambled down into the ditch and patted Earthy's hand.

The small scarecrow looked up at her gratefully.

'I'd sooner you went on looking for Worzel,' she answered. 'Hannah and me were going to have scoured Ten-acre, but most likely he's in the village. Hannah and me's shy about going there, so –'

'It's because we don't look so smart as what the other ladies do,' interrupted Hannah. 'We've not had their advantages. I'd like to look like that Mrs Bloomsbury-Barton, but I don't suppose she suffers from mice: that makes all the difference.'

Susan felt she must say something comforting, so she remarked, 'Mrs Braithewaite says Mrs Bloomsbury-Barton has a bee in her bonnet.'

'I've never had that,' said Hannah, who seemed to love talking about her own and other scarecrows' ailments. 'Not that, but I once had a friend who was a cruel sufferer from bees. She was ever so vain and she wore a straw bee skep instead of a bonnet. It looked smart enough until a swarm of bees came along and shared it with her. And another lady friend –'

But Earthy Mangold gave Hannah such a sharp little dig with her elbow that the rabbit jerked its ears up.

'I do wish you'd give over gossiping, Hannah. I never did hold with tittle-tattle. You just pull yourself together now.'

For the first time in the conversation Hannah Harrow answered quite sharply.

'The more I pulls myself together in one place the more the stuffing comes out in another, as you well know, Mrs Gummidge.'

'I think,' said Susan, who didn't want to be hindered by a scarecrow quarrel, 'I think we'd better go and look for Gummidge now.'

'I do wish you would,' replied Earthy. 'He's that impulsive you never know what he'll be up to next. You run along, my dears, and I'll get Hannah re-stuffed.'

But though John and Susan went to Ten-acre Field and looked over a great many hedges, they could not see Worzel Gummidge anywhere. There was no sign of him in the winding lane that led to Scatterbrook nor in the village street. But when they reached the Green they saw something that made them forget all about the scarecrow. The Vicar, the policeman, Mrs Bloomsbury-Barton and several other people were all walking about and prodding the snow with walking-sticks, rakes, and hoes.

'Whatever can they be doing?' asked Susan.

'Playing in the snow, I should think,' answered John.

'Silly! Would Mr Perkins play in the snow, or the policeman, *or* Mrs Bloomsbury-Barton?'

'Anyway, somebody's been making a snow man,' said John.

He was quite right. Standing in the middle of the village green was a very wide snow man.   It was a queer V shape and its hat was pulled so far over its face that it was almost resting on its pipe.

'Oh! I see,' said Susan. 'Let's make another one.'

But before John could either agree or disagree, Mrs Bloomsbury-Barton came bustling up to them.

'John! Susan! Come and join in the hunt, dears. Don't stand dawdling about. We must all try to help.'

For a moment Susan thought that everyone must be looking for Worzel Gummidge.

'Oh!' she said, 'are you looking for – for –?'

'Haven't you heard?' asked Mrs Bloomsbury-Barton. 'Surely you must have heard that dear Lady Lippindore, who is staying with me, has lost her beautiful pearl necklace. She is almost positive she dropped it here. You see, she always goes for a brisk walk before break-fast. She put the pearls on this morning, but when she came back to the house she had lost them. Come along and help, dears.'

'But we were looking for –' began Susan.

Luckily before she could mention Worzel Gummidge, the village policeman interrupted.

'See here,' he said. 'See here. We're not going to do any good by trampling over the snow like this. We'd have found the pearls by now if they were here. What we want is organization. Stand still, please, all of you. Now then, does everybody know that Lady Lippindore has offered a reward of five pounds to anyone who finds her pearls?'

There was a sort of happy murmur from everyone who heard.

'Well *then*,' went on the policeman, 'what we have to do is to *think*. We'll not do any good by tramping over the snow like a lot of silly chickens.'

Mrs Bloomsbury-Barton looked indignant, but then, of course, she was the only person present who was wearing a feathered hat.

'Really –' she began.

The policeman took no notice but continued his speech.

'People make mistakes sometimes and Lady Lippindore *may* have dropped the pearls somewhere else. Has anybody got any ideas?'

There was a long silence. Twice Mrs Bloomsbury-Barton opened and shut her mouth. Twice the Vicar coughed and then suddenly a very husky voice made an announcement –

'Look inside the statue!'

Everybody looked at everybody else. The Vicar coughed again. Somebody else coughed too; it was a sheep-like cough and very familiar to John and Susan.

'Who spoke?' asked the constable.

Once more there was a long pause and then the reply came in a sulky voice.

'How many more times do you want telling. Look inside the statue.'

Susan clutched John by the arm, as the constable stepped forward, and said:

'Will the person who made that announcement please speak up. Now then, my lad, don't be shy.'

Again came a pause and again an even surlier answer than the others had been –

'I have spoken up and I've said all I'm going to say.'

'Who said that?' asked the policemen.

'Sounded like Mr Kibbins' voice if you ask me,' said Mrs Higginsthwaite.

Mrs Kibbins contradicted her.

'Mr Kibbins is in bed with the influenza,' she snapped.

After that there was a great deal of argument while John and Susan looked anxiously round to see if Worzel Gummidge (for they both felt sure it was he who had spoken) could possibly be disguised as the policeman or the Vicar or Mr Higginsthwaite. But the faces of all the people were quite clean and not a bit turnipy. Nor was there the sign of a broomstick ankle peeping out from under any skirt or trouser-leg.

'Pearls in statues, the very idea!' said someone indignantly.

'There isn't a statue in Scatterbrook anyway,' said somebody else.

But a third person remembered that outside the Manor House that stood on the top of a hill beyond the village there was a statue of Colonel Wazenby-Gunthorpe. As nobody had any better suggestion and as the snow on the green was getting badly trampled and as everybody wanted the five pounds reward, the policeman led a procession along the road towards the Manor. John and Susan dodged behind a wall and let them go. They had something more important to look for.

CHAPTER XV

TAPIOCA PUDDING
—

'I *think* I know where Gummidge is,' whispered Susan, as the last of the searchers disappeared round a corner, 'I think I'm pretty well *certain* where he is because I saw smoke coming out of the snow-man's pipe.'

'Snow-men don't smoke,' said John.

'That's what I mean,' said Susan, 'but Gummidge might smoke.'

She jumped from her hiding-place behind the wall, ran across to the snow man and took off his hat. There, sticking up above a pair of very wide and snowy shoulders was Worzel Gummidge's turnip face. Except for the clay pipe in his mouth, he looked much the same as usual.

'So it *is* you!' cried Susan.

'Ooh aye!' agreed Gummidge.

John was too surprised to speak and, as Gummidge didn't seem to want to say anything, Susan asked the first question.

'What are you doing?'

'I'm being a statue,' was the answer. 'I'm being a statue in memory of Worzel Gummidge the Scarecrow of Scatterbrook. Rightly I didn't ought to be talking to you. Statues don't talk.'

'How did you get here?' asked John.

'Walked same as you did. But you'd best be off now. Don't you know it's rude to go runnin' about interruptin' statues?'

'We aren't running,' said Susan. 'We're standing as still as mice.'

Gummidge's pipe wobbled about in his mouth, as

he bit at the stem. Then he spoke in his angriest voice.

'There you go – reminding me about mice again. I tells you I'm fair sick o' mice. Nasty selfish things, that's what they are, always rustlin' about in folks' insides or taking the cheese out of other mice's mouse-traps. It's enough to make anybody sulk, so it is.'

Gummidge looked so dreadfully sulky that John interrupted him quickly.

'Please won't you tell us why you're being a statue.'

'I *am* telling you. I were just walking along thinking about them disappointed mice in Hannah Harrow's stummick when – ooh aye! It's enough to make anyone sulk.'

'But what happened?' asked Susan.

'I were walking along and I saw a nice string of pudding lying on the snow.'

'A string of WHAT?' asked John.

'A string of pudding. Leastways, I thought it was a string of tapioca pudding so I picks it up and puts it in my pocket. I had a nibble at it first, but it tasted a bit raw and then – and then I just chanced to sit down sudden. I was thinking how I could best get up when the school-children came along so I fell into a sulk like this.'

Gummidge closed his eyes and screwed up his mouth as he always did when he was sulking.

'Why did you fall into a sulk?' asked John softly when about two minutes had gone by.

'Wouldn't you sulk if children kept calling you an old scarecrow?' he asked.

'Well, but then I'm not a scarecrow.'

Gummidge opened the other eye.

'No more aren't I an *old* one. Bits of me's as young and younger nor what those children were. I've not had my fingers no more than eighteen months come Spring. So I just sulked at those children. And then they picked me up and set me down again and banked me up with snow till they'd made a statue of me. Good mornin'.'

Once more Gummidge shut his eyes, this time even more firmly than before. His pipe fell out of his mouth and the heat of it melted quite a deep hole in the snow, but still he did not speak.

'Oh dear!' said Susan at last. 'I'm afraid he's having a long sulk this time.'

'P'raps,' said John, 'P'raps he's only remembered that he's pretending to be a statue. He'll freeze to death though if he stays there much longer. Let's dig him out.'

Gummidge did not speak at all while John and Susan began to scrape the snow away from one side of him. It was hard work because it was still freezing, and their fingers soon began to ache as they scrabbled like terriers.

Presently they heard a ripping noise as Susan tore away at the hard snow round his pocket. A piece of frozen rag came away in her hand and all sorts of curious things came tumbling out into the snow. Among them were a banana skin, half a walnut, a knife-handle, a chunk of turnip, a button stuck to a piece of cheese AND a pearl necklace.

'Look!' said Susan, and she held it up. 'We'd better give this to Mrs Bloomsbury-Barton at once.'

'Robbers!' said Gummidge, and he opened his eyes. 'You leave my pockets be and stop meddling with what ain't yours.'

'But Gummidge, *dear*,' pleaded Susan. 'This is a string of real pearls.'

'Some calls it that. I calls it a string of artificial tapioca. Earthy'll call 'em what I do. They'll suit her too. Give 'em me back I say or I'll shout for the policeman.'

John and Susan looked at one another in despair. They knew there was always trouble whenever Gummidge became mixed up with other people.

'If Susan doesn't give them to Mrs Bloomsbury-

Barton you'll miss the five pounds reward,' said John.

'Five pounds o' what?'

'Well, just five pounds. You know, five pounds of five pounds.'

'Five pounds of mice most like. I know that Mrs Bloomsbury-Barton and how she rustles. Hannah rustles and she's full o' mice. That Mrs Bloomsbury-Barton rustles so it stands to reason she's full o' mice too.'

'I should think it's petticoats that make her rustle,' said Susan thoughtfully.

'Petticoats or mice – I don't want five pounds of either of 'em. I wants five pounds o' cheese or I'll keep that string of imitation tapioca pudding. She's coming back now. I'll ask her for the cheese. Put my hat on again, can't you, or she'll start throwing snowballs at me.'

Mrs Bloomsbury-Barton *was* coming back. The children had forgotten to watch the road, and now they saw that she was standing on the very edge of the Green itself. John put the hat back on to Gummidge's turnipy head only just in time, for Mrs Bloomsbury-Barton had seen them and was tip-toeing over the snow. She looked cold and very cross and the tip of her nose was quite blue.

'Please,' whispered Susan to Gummidge, 'Please don't speak to her.'

'I'll speak when I wants and I'll be a statue when I wants. So there!' The scarecrow's voice came thickly from under the felt hat, but he sounded very obstinate.

'We'll ask for the cheese. We'll do anything if only you'll go on being a statue,' begged Susan. And then Mrs Bloomsbury-Barton's voice interrupted her.

'John, Susan, I am surprised – more than surprised to find you playing with a snowman instead of helping us to look for the pearls.'

'But we've found them,' said John and he held out the gleaming string.

If Mrs Bloomsbury-Barton had not been such a fussily polite person it might have been said that she snatched at the pearls. Anyway, she took them very quickly and she did not seem to notice that they smelled of cheese.

'*How* did you find them?' she asked. '*Where* did you find them?'

The questions were rather difficult to answer. John did a good deal of pointing in the direction of the snowman. Susan did a good deal of talking about pockets and a friend and five pounds of cheese. The word 'cheese' seemed to worry Mrs Bloomsbury-Barton more than anything else.

'Cheese, my child,' she said as she led the way to her own house. 'Are you so fond of cheese?'

'Well, it's not exactly for us,' explained John.

'No, it's for a sort of friend of ours,' said Susan, very much wishing that grown-up people would not ask for so many reasons.

'For some poor person do you mean, dear?'

'I don't think he's exactly rich,' answered Susan.

'Rich!' John repeated, 'Rich, I don't think he's got any money at all.'

Mrs Bloomsbury-Barton made a sort of clicking sound with her tongue, and then asked.

'What is the poor man's name, dear?'

'It's Wor –' began Susan, but John kicked her so hard that she ended up by saying, 'It's Wor – *you* know, but I think I'd better not say what his name is.'

'No, you'd better not,' put in John.

Mrs Bloomsbury-Barton smiled at them in an approving sort of way, and nodded her head as people do nod heads when they think they know something that nobody else understands.

'No doubt the poor fellow is poor but proud.'

Susan gave a little gulp because it was so difficult to

think of Worzel Gummidge being proud, but she managed to finish her gulps by the time Mrs Bloomsbury-Barton had finished saying – 'Poor but proud – that shows a noble spirit. And you are dear unselfish children. John, dear, while Susan comes into the house with me, will you run up to the Manor and tell the policeman that we have found the pearls.'

So, while Susan followed Mrs Bloomsbury-Barton to her house, John, after glancing at the snow-covered scarecrow, ran up the lane that led to the top of the hill. It did not take him very long, and when he had given the message he raced back for fear anyone should overtake him.

When he reached the Green, Susan, who was carrying a basket, came out of Mrs Bloomsbury-Barton's house.

She didn't see John for a moment or two. He didn't see her either because they were both staring at the heap of dirty melted snow that had once covered Worzel Gummidge, the scarecrow.

'Where has he gone?' asked Susan at last, but John couldn't tell her and there was nobody else to ask.

'He can't just have melted,' said John. 'He couldn't. People, I mean scarecrows, don't just melt.'

Susan's voice was dismal.

'All the same, it looks awfully like the melt that Gummidge would make if he *did* melt. Look how *black* the snow is. Oh! I do wish Gummidge wasn't so disappearing and sudden.'

John stooped down and picked up the clay pipe. The sight of it nearly made Susan cry. Her voice was quite choky, as she said, 'Oh! poor Gummidge. And I've got his cheese here in this basket. And Mrs Bloomsbury-Barton gave me some tea and sugar and things too. What had we better do with them?'

'Take them back to Hannah and Earthy, I should

think,' said John. 'After all the cheese is for Hannah Harrow.'

'For Hannah's *mice*,' corrected Susan.

So they went back by the way they had come, and it seemed much longer because the basket was so bumpy and prickly against their legs. The snow squeaked a little and the basket creaked, but everything else was silent. They felt too miserable to speak to each other until after they had passed the ditch where they had left Hannah and Earthy. Only some scuffled snow, a sad little heap of sawdust and a tarry strand of Hannah's hair told them that the scarecrows had ever been there at all. But when they had climbed the hedge they followed a very scruffled trail through the snow towards the haystack.

'It looks rather as though Hannah had been a bit heavy to carry,' remarked John. 'Poor Earthy.'

'Poor Earthy! Poor Hannah! Poor Gummidge,' agreed Susan. 'Oh! I do think scarecrows lead the most awfully sad lives. They're always coming to bits and –'

'The haystack looks as though it's coming to bits,' said John, as they reached Earthy's home. 'I wonder if anyone's at home.'

'I suppose it would be polite to knock,' said Susan, 'but it's a bit difficult to knock at a haystack.'

However, there was no need to knock, for the familiar sheep-like cough told them that Gummidge was at home. So did the voice of Earthy who seemed to be singing a sort of lullaby: –

> '*Hushaby, Gummidge,*
> *My best bit of rummidge,*
>   *Hushaby Gummidge, my pet.*
> *Tatter and raggle*
> *And coat in a draggle*
>   *Gummidge so queer and so wet –*'

'I never knew Earthy could sing,' exclaimed Susan.
'I'm not sure that she can now,' said John. 'Listen.'
Earthy went on singing: –

> *'Hushaby, Gummidge,*
> *My best bit of rummidge,*
> *Hannah and Earthy are here.*
>
> *Gummidge, my tattered*
> *And Gummidge, my spattered,*
> *Worzel, my dainty, my dear.'*

'*If* he's dainty,' said Susan, 'if he's *dainty*, he must have
changed in a very great hurry. Let's peep into the
haystack and see what's happening.'

The sight they saw was worth seeing. At the entrance to
the tunnel leading into the haystack lay something that
looked like a huge and rather shaggy hedgehog. Bristles
of straw stuck up from it in every direction and only the
turnip head with the green sprouting hair showed that it
was Worzel Gummidge, the scarecrow. His eyes were
tightly shut, his face was very damp but he was still
smiling. Sitting beside him, and wringing out a pair of
wet ragged trousers over her own skirt was Earthy Mangold. Hannah Harrow, looking much plumper but a
great deal lumpier, was wringing out Gummidge's coat.

'Earthy!' cried Susan.

Earthy put a twig-like finger to her lips and said,
'Hush! He's sleeping peaceful and no wonder after what
he's been through.'

'We were so afraid he might have melted,' whispered
Susan.

'Anyone'd melt,' said Earthy, 'if they'd had three
buckets of doorstep water throwed at 'em by Mrs
Kibbins.'

'Is that what happened after we went away?'

'That's what happened, sure enough, my dear.'

Earthy squeezed some drops of muddy water on to Gummidge's face. 'Why can't people leave innocent snow statues alone and not go throwing water at them, that's what I say. I'm sorry I can't ask you in just now, but we're in a bit of an upset, as you can see.'

The children could see that quite plainly. Some cheese rind, a lot of old tins and remnants of sacking had been added to the other rubbish that littered the outside of the hayrick.

'Oh! we won't come in, thank you,' said John. 'But do tell me what Gummidge did when Mrs Kibbins threw the water at him?'

'Shook himself like a cat's paw that's trod in a puddle, and walked home. All chattering and shivering he were and talking about a string of tapioca pudding and five pounds of cheese.'

Susan remembered the basket, and put it down.

'We've got the cheese,' she said, 'and lots of other things as well.'

'Ooh aye!' muttered Gummidge, and he opened one eye. 'Leave 'em be and leave me be too.'

'You might say thank you,' said John.

'I'm an invalid – that's what I am. Invalids don't say thank you. Invalids just goes to sleep and sulks.'

'But you can't sulk in your sleep,' said Susan. Gummidge shut his eye and did not speak, but Earthy answered.

'That's just what he can do. Mr Gummidge has a great gift for sulking.'

CHAPTER XVI

THE CHRISTMAS PARTY

—

IT was a few days before Christmas and Scatterbrook village school was filled with rather gloomy children who were all wearing their Sunday clothes and very little of their weekday grubbiness. Mrs Bloomsbury-Barton was in charge of the annual Christmas party. But though the desks had been pushed back against the walls and a few sprigs of holly were decorating the maps and blackboard, somehow the schoolroom did not look or smell a bit Christmassy. It still looked like a schoolroom and it smelled of carbolic and india-rubber and chalk and red ink and very dull books. And Mrs Bloomsbury-Barton seemed to be even more like a school-mistress than the teacher who was sitting by the old piano.

John and Susan, who had just come into the room, heard her arguing with Tommy Higginsthwaite.

'No, Tommy,' she said, 'we are *not* going to have a Christmas Tree this year. Emmeline's dress caught fire last time when the candles flared up.'

'Bother!' whispered Susan. 'I do love the smell of Christmas Tree candles just when they've been snuffed out, and I do love all the glittery things.'

'And I do wish we hadn't come,' said John. 'I hate parties.'

Then Mrs Bloomsbury-Barton saw them, so they had to shake hands though it was rather painful because she wore so many rings and her fingers were bony. After that she beckoned to them to follow her, and they stood waiting rather sulkily while she put her finger to her lips in a mysterious sort of way.

'Listen, dears,' she said, 'I feel sure you will help me, so I am going to tell you a great great secret. Father Christmas is coming to visit us to-night. Not the *real* Father Christmas, but Major Wazenby-Gunthorpe who is staying with his cousins at the Manor House. I don't know him, but I am told that he always helps to make any party go. Dear dear! what a terrible noise! Gently,

gently, Tommy Higginsthwaite. Little boys should make way for little girls. Hush! Hush! Hush!'

After Mrs Bloomsbury-Barton had finished making hushing noises like a shunting train and had separated two little girls who were pulling each other's hair, she came back to the place where Susan and John were waiting. Then she explained that as soon as three knocks were heard on the door Susan was to open it and John was to exclaim, 'Why! I do believe it's Father Christmas!'

'But supposing it isn't?' asked John.

'Nonsense, dear, of course it will be. I mean, of course it will *really* be Major Wazenby-Gunthorpe with a sack of presents.'

'Presents,' said Susan. 'How lovely!'

'Yes, dear, but never mind about the presents now. When John has made his little speech I want you to say, "Good evening, Father Christmas. Did you come down the chimney?" Speak up clearly, dear, and try not to be shy. Can you do that?'

'Yes,' said Susan, 'only, only I mean, there's only a stove in this room. There isn't a chimney at all and – and they all know there isn't.'

'Try not to be babyish, dear,' replied Mrs Bloomsbury-Barton. She might have said more but just then Tommy Higginsthwaite tucked Willy Wiseman's head under his arm and began to punch it.

Mrs Bloomsbury-Barton bustled away.

A few minutes later, John and Susan heard the tune of 'Oranges and Lemons' being thumped out on the piano, but they could only just hear it because the children were making such a noise and shouting the song at the tops of their voices.

'I wonder what sort of Christmas Gummidge is having,' said Susan. 'And I wonder if scarecrows hang up their stockings.'

John looked doubtful. 'Anyway they can't *all* hang up stockings because quite a lot of them haven't any,' he said.

Susan remembered poor little Upsidaisy's pair of stocking tops, and was just going to speak when there came a knock on the door.

It was really only the whisper of a knock, but it was repeated three times, so she opened the door.

A very curious looking person was standing just outside. He was wearing a sort of bonnet that seemed to be made out of a red woollen scarf. A crimson motor-rug was draped round his shoulders, and he was carrying a bulging sack. He was quite a little man and he looked very puzzled and worried.

'Why!' began John in a loud voice, 'I do believe –'

But before he could say anything more the queer little man put a hand on his arm, and said, 'Wait a bit, boy. Wait a bit. Tell me, do I look like Father Christmas?'

'Well, not *very*,' John told him.

''Fraid not! 'Fraid not! 'Fraid not. But I did the best I could.'

He sounded so worried that Susan did her best to cheer him up.

'The rug's a lovely colour, but you'd look better if you had a white beard and a red flannel dressing-gown.'

'I know that. I know that. I know that!' The children noticed that the strange Father Christmas generally repeated everything three times.

'I know that! I had a beard and a dressing-gown, but they both disappeared out of the back of the car. I had to stop to change a wheel – not half a mile from here. Somebody must have stolen my clothes then. Most annoying.'

'But you've got your sack anyway,' said Susan in a comforting voice.

'Got that! Got that! But it's all covered with mud and it was perfectly clean when I left home. As a matter of fact, I did see a gawky-looking fellow walking along the road. I overtook him before I punctured. Perhaps he stole my things.'

'Was he very gawky-looking?' asked Susan because a dreadful idea had come into her head.

'Gawky? Yes, looked like a scarecrow.'

'I wonder –' began John.

Just then the music stopped and Mrs Bloomsbury-Barton left the shouting children at the other end of the room and bustled towards the door.

'Why!' she said in a shrill unnatural voice, 'I do believe we have an unexpected visitor. I really think it must be Father Christmas. Come in, Father Christmas; we are all ready to welcome you. Children, children, it really is Father Christmas. At least –'

As Mrs Bloomsbury-Barton finished speaking, the man in the queer clothes came shyly into the room. He looked even odder than he had done at first because the muddy sack he was carrying was now making marks all over his coat; and the motor-rug was slipping from his shoulders so that it trailed at the back like a train. His face was almost as red as the scarf round his head. Before he could say a word to Mrs Bloomsbury-Barton he was surrounded by children.

They pushed and they pulled. They stuck elbows into each other's eyes and they breathed down the red neck of Father Christmas.

'Stand back, dears,' said Mrs Bloomsbury-Barton. 'Stand back and let Father Christmas have some room. Look, he is going to open the sack now.'

Father Christmas was breathing very heavily as he tugged and pulled at the tarred muddy string that was tied tightly round the mouth of the sack. At last, when he had broken two finger-nails and covered his hands with tar, he managed to undo the knot.

'Now!' said Mrs Bloomsbury-Barton to a small girl who was crying. 'Now, watch, Mary, and see what's coming out of the sack. I am sure it will be something pretty!'

It *was* something pretty, but it was not anything that Mrs Bloomsbury-Barton or anybody else had expected, for there was a sudden movement near the top of the sack and out hopped a small rabbit. It bounced against Mary's face and then scuttled to the end of the room, where it crouched under a desk.

'Good gracious me!' said the strange Father Christmas. '*What* a queer thing to find in a sack.'

All the children opened and shut their mouths – that is to say all except Mary, who left hers open and bellowed.

Only the rabbit seemed to be unsurprised. It sat up under the desk and began to wash its face and sleek its quivering whiskers.

'I think it's Gummidge's rabbit,' said Susan. She had to speak loudly because Mary was roaring and Mrs Bloomsbury-Barton was pleading with her to stop – 'Look at the pretty little rabbit. We didn't know Father Christmas was a conjurer, did we?'

'Conjurer!' muttered Father Christmas. 'Conjurer indeed!' If the rabbit had been a dragon he could not have looked more worried.

'Yes, and a very clever conjurer,' said Mrs Bloomsbury-Barton brightly. 'Now, Father Christmas, can you do another funny trick to cheer Mary up? Perhaps you can take sixpence out of her hair or something?'

'Certainly not! Certainly not!'

'Then I'm sure you'll be able to find a lovely present for her in the sack.' Mrs Bloomsbury-Barton spoke quickly because, although Mary had stopped roaring and was now licking up the tears that ran down her left cheek, she might begin again at any moment.

Father Christmas stooped down towards the sack and as he did so the red scarf slipped over his eyes. He did not wait to push it back but fumbled in the sack, pulled something out, and pushed it in the direction of Mary. The something was an old, a very old turnip.

Mary answered him more loudly than before and continued to roar while Mrs Bloomsbury-Barton explained that Father Christmas was really a most wonderful conjurer and that it was all a joke.

Mary refused to see the joke.

'Perhaps,' said Mrs Bloomsbury-Barton, 'perhaps it would be better if you were to stop playing tricks, Father Christmas. Mary is rather over-wrought. After all, she is only a tiny mite. Now, Mary, dry those tears and watch Father Christmas. I wonder what he is going to take out of the sack *this* time.'

'Something that doesn't smell very nice,' announced Tommy Higginsthwaite.

'Hush, Tommy, or Father Christmas won't find anything for you.'

But Tommy was right, for the empty sardine tin, which was now pulled out of the sack, did not smell at all nice.

'Can't understand it,' said the strange Father Christmas. 'Can't understand it, can't understand it at all.' As he spoke he went on pulling queer things out of the sack. Some broken gramophone records came first, then a perambulator wheel and then a brick.

The children began to mutter now:–

'It's a shame, so it is.'

'Saying we were going to have a surprise.'

'Look at all that dirty rubbish.'

Mrs Bloomsbury-Barton tried to quieten them by saying, 'Hush! Hush! Don't be rude, children. Father Christmas is only playing tricks on you.'

'Tricks!' muttered Father Christmas, 'Tricks indeed. Now what in the world is this? OW!'

'Oh dear!' exclaimed Mrs Bloomsbury-Barton. 'What is the matter?' For Father Christmas had jerked his hand out of the sack and was now sucking his finger.

'Hurt my hand on something. Yes, it's barbed wire. Never heard such a thing in my life. Look!'

He put his left hand back into the sack, then pulled out a length of rusty barbed wire.

'This is a bit too much,' he said. 'I'm not going to risk being caught in barbed wire entanglements or bitten by rabbits or rats. I'll tip up the sack.'

While he raised the sack by its two bottom corners Mrs Bloomsbury-Barton spoke brightly to the angry children.

'Isn't Father Christmas being *funny*. Now for the big big surprises. I expect all the lovely presents are at the bottom of the sack.'

Surprises did indeed tumble from the sack as the furious-looking Father Christmas jerked and heaved.

Out came orange peel, banana skins, a last year's bird's-nest, an empty ginger-beer bottle, bits of turnip, potatoes, carrots, half a skipping rope, a horseshoe and some rusty nails.

There was silence for a moment or two; and then a couple of children began to cry, while another one said it was a shame and she would tell her mother.

All the while the rabbit went on washing its face and whiskers. John looked at it and so did Susan.

'I'm going to catch the rabbit,' said John. 'We don't want anybody to frighten it.'

But all the other children seemed to have forgotten about the rabbit. They were playing with the queer rubbish that had fallen out of the sack and were getting so rusty and sticky and tarry and turnipy and muddy that Mrs Bloomsbury-Barton begged them to put every-thing back into the sack. She told them that she and Father Christmas were going to have a quiet little talk together, and that he would very soon come back with a clean sack filled with lovely surprises.

So while she and the strange Father Christmas walked across the school-room and out through the doorway, John and Susan went softly towards the rabbit.

It was not at all difficult to catch. In fact, it gave only one little hop before John caught it. After that it sat in Susan's lap, quivered its nose, and let her play with its long ears.

'I suppose,' said John, 'I suppose it must be Gummidge's rabbit.'

'Of course,' agreed Susan. 'And of course, that was Gummidge's sack – at least it's the sort of sack he would have. And the things looked like the sort of things he would put into a sack.'

John scowled as he answered, 'Well, if he's stolen the other sack *and* the Father Christmas clothes, it's too bad of him.'

'But Gummidge always *is* being too bad.'

The rabbit turned its head away as Susan spoke and when she stroked it again gave her quite a sharp little nip. Evidently it was a loyal rabbit.

'We're always getting into rows because of him,' said John. 'But they always come right in the end.'

The rabbit flopped up its ears and then gave a little hop that took him from Susan's lap to John's knees. It sat there quite quietly and did not move anything except its whiskers when the school teacher at the piano began to strum out the tune of Nuts-in-May.

'Let's go and play,' said Susan.

'How can we play Nuts-in-May with a rabbit?' asked John.

'No, I suppose we can't. Let's take him back to the farm first. We can always come back afterwards. I've got a sort of feeling that this is going to be one of our Gummidgy days.'

But before John and Susan could reach the door they were met by Mrs Bloomsbury-Barton who was just hurrying back into the school-room and looking very worried indeed.

CHAPTER XVII

GUMMIDGE'S REINDEER

—

'A DREADFUL thing has happened, my dears,' she said. 'It seems that Major Wazenby-Gunthorpe was not joking at all when he took all those dreadful things out of that terrible sack. He was just as puzzled as we were.'

'Yes, I know,' said John.

Mrs Bloomsbury-Barton looked at him suspiciously, and then snapped:

'Well, if you knew, why didn't you say so?'

'There wasn't much chance.' John shuffled from one foot to another.

'He told us about it,' interrupted Susan. 'He said somebody had stolen his clothes and that the sack was all muddy and – and –'

She stopped because Mrs Bloomsbury-Barton was looking so annoyed, and then added, 'I'm sure he only did it for a sort of joke – the person who took the sack, I mean.'

'A very poor sort of joke!' Mrs Bloomsbury-Barton tossed her head until her earrings made little tinkly sounds. 'At any rate, Major Wazenby-Gunthorpe has driven back to the Manor to see if he can find the thief.'

'Oh dear!' said Susan, and then wished, as she so often did, that she had not spoken at all.

'Why do you say that?'

'She means,' said John, making things much worse, 'that she hopes he won't catch whoever did it.'

'How can you say such a thing. The man who stole poor dear little children's toys deserves to go to prison. We must hope for the best. Now if you want to help you will stay by the door again.'

'Why do you want us to?' asked Susan. 'Is Major Wazenby-Gunthorpe coming back again?'

Mrs Bloomsbury-Barton explained that though Major Wazenby-Gunthorpe would not be able to come back as he had to go to London that evening he hoped to send a friend instead.

'That is,' she said, 'if he is able to find the lost clothes and the sack of presents. If not we shall all have to be very jolly and cheerful and make the best of everything.'

Then Mrs Bloomsbury-Barton bustled off to stop a fight between two little boys, and John and Susan were left standing by the door. It was very dull so they were glad that they had the rabbit to keep them company. At least, it was dull until they heard a coughing noise from outside.

'Listen,' said Susan, 'that sounds like Gummidge's cough.'

'Nonsense!' answered John, 'you've got Gummidge on the brain! How *could* he be here?'

'You never know where Gummidge will be.'

Susan was quite right. There was a thump on the door, and then it was pushed open. A strange figure, in a crimson woollen dressing-gown bordered with cotton wool, walked sideways into the school-room. Its face was almost covered by a huge white beard. It wore a red hood, and carried a sack over one shoulder; on its hands were motoring gauntlets.

'Gummidge!' cried John, for no clothes could ever really disguise Worzel Gummidge.

''Taint Gummidge. It's Father Christmas.'

'But why have you come?' asked Susan.

'I've come a'cos I weren't invited – that's why. I'd heard tell of this party and I wasn't *not* going to come.'

John tried to stand in the way, but Worzel Gummidge pushed past him, muttering, 'I've got the presents and I've got the right clothes. I took 'em out of a motycar that stopped on the road. I'm going to go round catching people and filling their stockings, if they'll stand still long enough.'

'But you *can't*,' said Susan in a horrified voice. 'You can't fill stockings when people have got them on.'

Gummidge shook himself impatiently and took two more shuffling steps.

'That's all you knows about it. The fuller they are of leg, the easier they are to fill, 'cos they don't hold so much. Ooh aye! 'Evenin'. Merry Christmas!'

Gummidge shouted the last words so loudly that Mrs Bloomsbury-Barton heard him and came almost running across the school-room. She seized Gummidge's gaunt-leted hand, shook it happily, and said, 'So all's well that ends well. How quick you have been. I could almost believe you have come down the chimney.'

Gummidge muttered that he wasn't a chimney-sweep, but Mrs Bloomsbury-Barton did not seem to hear. She clapped her hands and called to all the children to come and see what Father Christmas had brought for them. Some of them came rather shyly at first and Mary had to be dragged along by her elder sister because the sight of a bulging sack had made her cry again.

'Dear! Dear! I hope the child is not going to make another scene,' said Mrs Bloomsbury-Barton.

'Makes more of a sound than a scene!' said Gummidge. 'Make a fine rook-scarer she would. I've a mind to set her up in Ten-acre till Spring when rooks is busiest. She'd keep 'em off.'

Gummidge sidled towards Mary, who began to bellow more loudly than ever. John tried to pull him back, and Mrs Bloomsbury-Barton patted Mary's head in a despairing sort of way.

'Now dry those tears, dear. Father Christmas was only joking.'

'She'd be no joke to the rooks!' said Gummidge. 'She'd –'

Mrs Bloomsbury-Barton interrupted him.

'Perhaps Mary could have her present first. After all she is only a tiny mite.'

'I've known scarecrows twice her size that couldn't make half o' that noise. It's as good as a nanny-goat.'

Gummidge dumped down the sack and gave it a kick which sent two large chunks of mud flying from his boots.

'Dear me,' said Mrs Bloomsbury-Barton, looking down at his feet. 'I am afraid you must have had a terribly muddy journey, Father Christmas. Did you walk?'

'Ooh aye! But I never knocks the mud off of my boots in winter: it makes 'em so much thicker. I knocks it off in the summer now and again.'

Mrs Bloomsbury-Barton looked puzzled as she murmured, 'What an original idea!'

Another lump of mud fell from Gummidge's forehead and dropped to the floor, when he heaved up the heavy sack by the corners and emptied the contents on to the floor. There were toy trains, books, dolls, games, paint-boxes, and all sorts of lovely presents.

'Take what you likes,' said Gummidge, and he stirred

up the heap of toys with his muddiest boot. 'Ooh aye! Take what you likes. Don't keep bothering me to choose.' Then he bent down jerkily, and snatched up a rattle. 'You can't have that though, I wants it.'

Gummidge shook the rattle so near to Mrs Bloomsbury-Barton's face that she had to dodge back a little. Gummidge followed her, and John and Susan followed him.

They would have liked to have chosen some presents too, but they were very anxious about Worzel Gummidge, so they left the other children to blow trumpets and wind up mechanical toys and fight and scramble.

'And now,' asked Mrs Bloomsbury-Barton brightly, as Gummidge stopped twirling the rattle, 'how is everybody up at the Manor?'

'Couldn't say, I'm sure,' said Gummidge carelessly.

'But surely you came from there?'

'I came from home, but I'm not there now, so it's no good asking me how anyone is. Hannah she were in a bad way when I left.'

Mrs Bloomsbury-Barton made sympathetic clucking noises. 'Dear! Dear! And is Hannah a child?'

'Not she, nor never were!' was the surprising answer. 'She were made out of old stuff to start with.'

'What an amusing way of putting things. I always say that some children are born old. I hope she is not very ill.'

'She's not ill at all,' said Gummidge. 'She's gone and lost a finger.'

'Lost a finger!' exclaimed Mrs Bloomsbury-Barton. 'How terrible. However did it happen? What a ghastly accident!'

John and Susan very much hoped that Gummidge would not answer the question because they were so afraid that he would say something to show he was not a human being, but he went on happily.

"Tweren't an accident. 'Twere done on purpose!'

Mrs Bloomsbury-Barton looked horrified.

'Ooh aye! 'Twere done on purpose. A friend got annoyed and stamped on it. They'd been having a bit of a quarrel so the friend up and jumped, and now Hannah's that peevish there's no doing anything with her. I says to her before I leaves home, I says, "What's the use of scrabbling about lookin' for lost fingers when you've got eight or nine on each hand as 'tis?" '

Mrs Bloomsbury-Barton, who had been looking more and more alarmed, now smiled brightly.

'Now I understand that you are joking,' she said.

'Sometimes I jokes and sometimes I don't. Lots of funny things happens to me.'

'You must tell the children about them,' said Mrs Bloomsbury-Barton. 'Perhaps you can tell them some funny stories while John and Susan help me to carry the crackers from Mrs Kibbins' cottage. That will be splendid.'

'Ooh aye!' said Gummidge, and he shuffled his way towards the noisy children while John and Susan followed Mrs Bloomsbury-Barton out of the schoolroom. They went across the yard and down the road towards Mrs Kibbins' cottage; and all the time they were dreadfully afraid that, while they were away, Worzel Gummidge would do something funny that they would miss or something terrible that they ought to stop.

'Anyway,' said John, as Mrs Bloomsbury-Barton bustled up the path to the cottage door. 'Anyway, she doesn't seem to have noticed anything so far. She only thinks Gummidge is trying to be funny; so that's all right.'

'But I don't think Gummidge *can* go on being all right,' objected Susan. 'Oh! I do hope Mrs Bloomsbury-Barton will be quick.'

But Mrs Bloomsbury-Barton was a very long time. She was so long that John and Susan felt very inclined to run back to the school and see what was happening to Gummidge. They stood by the wall and watched the shadows on the blind and scuffled their feet on the frosty path. Presently Mr Kibbins rode up on his bicycle, got off, pushed it into a shed and went into the cottage. But still Mrs Bloomsbury-Barton did not appear. When at last she did, the children could hear from her agitated breathing that something had gone wrong. She seemed to have forgotten all about the crackers too.

'We must go back to the school at once,' she said. 'A terrible thing has happened. Mr Kibbins is going straight off to telephone for the police.'

'For the police?' repeated Susan, 'Oh! but why?'

'Because Mr Kibbins has just come back from the Manor with a message to say that the sack and the clothes could not be found. That means that the strange man in the school-room is only pretending to be Father Christmas. The people at the Manor know nothing about him at all.'

There was a pause because neither John nor Susan could think of anything to say. Mrs Bloomsbury-Barton continued:

'I thought the man's manner was peculiar and so were his boots. He may be a burglar.'

'But,' argued Susan miserably, 'he was *giving* presents away – not stealing them.'

'He must have stolen them in the first place,' snapped Mrs Bloomsbury-Barton.

'But he's giving them back now,' said John. 'I don't want him to be put in prison.'

'Don't be childish,' said Mrs Bloomsbury-Barton.

Very, very sadly John and Susan followed her back to the school, and crept up to the group of children who were surrounding Gummidge. He was sitting on the floor, and all round him, busy with penknives and scissors from new work-baskets, were the children. They were hacking pieces off the front of his red flannel dressing-gown, though there was not very much left of it. Some of the children were cutting smaller pieces into tiny squares, and Gummidge was tweaking the cotton-wool trimming into tufts. As he worked he sang:

> *'Christmas comes but once a year,*
> *Rabbits wants new scuts to weer.*
> *Robins what've got no vests*
> *Needs some flannel for their chests.'*

When he had finished singing he tugged at a piece of his cotton-wool beard, jerked his head back and saw John and Susan.

'We're getting ready for the Christmas tree,' he announced happily. 'Ooh aye! we're going to have a fine Christmas tree up in the spinney by Ten-acre. The hen robins will be that pleased when they see their new chest-protectors, they'll fly backwards. Come and help, can't you?'

But before John and Susan could move, Mrs Blooms-bury-Barton grabbed each of them by a wrist.

'Don't go near him, my dears,' she whispered. 'He is quite mad, poor creature. On no account contradict him.'

'I can't hear a word you're saying,' complained Gummidge.

Mrs Bloomsbury-Barton stretched her mouth until she almost looked as though she were smiling. She gripped John's wrist and Susan's left one so tightly that she quite hurt, but they did not mind because they felt sorry for her. They longed to explain who Gum-midge really was but they knew they would never be believed.

'Don't you think it would be a good idea if we were all

to have a jolly game of Nuts-in-May,' she asked as brightly as possible. She glanced towards the piano, but the school teacher had gone.

'Nuts-in-May!' shouted Gummidge so fiercely that Mrs Bloomsbury-Barton let go of John and Susan and moved backwards.

'Yes, the game, you know,' she said soothingly, and began to sing in a quavering voice:

> '*Here we come gathering Nuts-in-May*
> *On a cold and frosty morning.*'

'Daft!' said Gummidge rudely, 'daft – that's what you are. Nuts aren't ripe in May; you don't get 'em till the autumn. An' it isn't May either no more than it's mornin'.'

He wrenched another tuft from his beard while Mrs Bloomsbury-Barton whispered. 'That shows he is mad. Mad people always think that other people are mad, you know.'

'Nuts-in-May,' repeated Gummidge. 'It'll be Christmas roses in June next.'

'It's only a game, you know,' explained Susan. 'A game like – like Hunt-the-slipper, you know.'

'I don't know!' Gummidge snatched the scissors from Tommy Higginsthwaite and chopped up another strip of red flannel.

'Folks don't hunt slippers, no, nor boots either. They hunts foxes and hares. Seems everyone's turning daft. What's it matter though? I feels that reckless I don't care what I does.'

'Oh dear, dear!' whispered Mrs Bloomsbury-Barton. 'I do wish the police would come or a doctor or some- body.'

As though in answer to her wish, there was a bumping noise and the door at the other end of the room opened.

As a matter of fact, John had forgotten to shut it properly.

'That'll be my reindeer!' remarked Gummidge as a large animal walked into the room. But the creature that came meandering along as quietly as though it were returning to its stall was not a reindeer, but a cow. At least, it looked like a cow, even though it was wearing a piece of mistletoe on one horn.

Everyone, even Mrs Bloomsbury-Barton and even Tommy Higginsthwaite, was too surprised to speak. It didn't seem as though it could possibly be true. Cows do not come to Christmas parties and stand swishing their tails and mooing. Neither do two dozen people usually share the same dream.

'Have to be off now,' said Gummidge.

Still nobody spoke. Nobody moved either except the rabbit which suddenly hopped from John's pocket and went lolloping across the floor to join scraps of red flannel and tufts of wool in Worzel Gummidge's dressing-gown pocket. He patted it gently, then picked up the empty sack, sat astride it and grasped the cow's tail.

'Anybody else coming for a ride?' he asked. 'Anybody else coming to my Christmas tree?'

Still nobody answered, and the cow took a few steps towards the door.

'Merry Christmas! Merry Christmas!' shouted Gummidge. 'It's been a lovely Christmas Eve. You can have what's left of the beard. Earthy likes me medium-shaved best!'

Away went the cow with Gummidge hanging on to its tail. Away went Gummidge's cotton-wool beard as he flung it towards Mrs Bloomsbury-Barton. Out of his pocket popped the rabbit's head and then popped back again. Out of the door went the cow and Gummidge and all the school-children and Mrs Bloomsbury-Barton and John and Susan.

They were just in time to see Worzel Gummidge being jerked round the corner in the moonlight.

'His poor clothes,' said Susan, as she picked up the sack which Gummidge must have left in a very great hurry.

'Let's go back to the farm now,' said John. 'I'm a bit tired of this party.'

'I wish we could go to Gummidge's party though,' said Susan. 'We shan't see him again for ages and ages because we go home to-morrow.'

But they did see him again before they left Scatter-brook. In fact, they saw him that very night when they stopped to look out of the landing window at the shining roofs of Scatterbrook.

'What a lovely moon,' said Susan. 'I wonder if the scarecrows are enjoying their party.'

Suddenly somebody coughed huskily in the yard below. Gummidge was looking up at the window.

'Evenin',' he said. 'I've brought your Christmas presents. There's a lock of Hannah's hair, from Hannah and a hollyberry necklace from Earthy and some straw boots from me. Merry Christmas!'

'Merry Christmas!' said John.

'Merry Christmas!' said Susan.

Gummidge stooped down and laid his presents by the farm-yard pump. Then he waved a gawky arm at them and shambled out of the yard.

It all happened so quickly that they could scarcely believe it had happened at all, but when they went out in the morning there were two bottle-straws, a length of tarred string and a hollyberry necklace.

'I don't suppose anyone else in the world has ever had a Christmas present from a scarecrow before,' said Susan.